MW01222749

River
of Gold

River
of Gold

A Novel

Susan Dobbie

RONSDALE PRESS

RIVER OF GOLD
Copyright © 2009 Susan Dobbie

All rights reserved. No part of this publication may be reproduced, stored in a retrieval system, or transmitted, in any form or by any means, without prior written permission of the publisher, or, in Canada, in the case of photocopying or other reprographic copying, a licence from Access Copyright (Canadian Copyright Licensing Agency).

RONSDALE PRESS
3350 West 21st Avenue
Vancouver, B.C., Canada
v6s 1G7

Typesetting: Julie Cochrane in Fairfield Light 11 pt on 16.5
Cover Design: Nancy de Brouwer, Alof!i Graphic Design
Paper: Ancient Forest Friendly "Silva" (FSC) — 100% post-consumer waste, totally chlorine-free

Ronsdale Press wishes to thank the following for their support of its publishing program: the Canada Council for the Arts, the Government of Canada through the Book Publishing Industry Development Program (BPIDP), the British Columbia Arts Council, and the Province of British Columbia through the British Columbia Book Publishing Tax Credit program.

Library and Archives Canada Cataloguing in Publication

Dobbie, Susan (date)
   River of gold / Susan Dobbie.

ISBN 978-1-55380-071-2

   1. Cariboo (B.C.: Regional district) — Gold discoveries — Fiction. I. Title.

PS8557.021 R58 2009   c813'.6   C2009-900689-8

At Ronsdale Press we are committed to protecting the environment. To this end we are working with Markets Initiative (www.oldgrowthfree.com) and printers to phase out our use of paper produced from ancient forests. This book is one step towards that goal.

Printed in Canada by Marquis Printing, Quebec

To Kristin, Lara, Trevor, Andrew,
Ceilidh, Alexander, Kimberley
and Adriana

ACKNOWLEDGEMENTS

I WISH TO THANK MY publisher, Ronald B. Hatch, for his direction and guidance through the writing of this book. I am in his debt. I also thank my husband Hugh for his ongoing support of my solitary writing habit. The Langley Centennial Museum must also be thanked for allowing me the privilege of working as a docent for the past thirteen years, and for feeding my curiosity about our province's history.

River
of Gold

chapter one

THEY CALL ME KANAKA. *Human being*, it means in Hawaiian. Soon I'll be forty. And I'll have lived half my life in this place.

On the north side of the Fraser River, opposite the Langley fort, towards the back of a clearing hewn out years ago, there's a small wooden shack, one of a ramshackle row, sitting second from the end. In this small pocket in the cloak of time, it belongs to me, Kimo Maka Kanui. A new world is taking shape around me. Some of it I understand; some I never will. There are my far-off islands in the Pacific, the earth's scattered continents, and my workplace, the Langley fort across the river, named for a far-off Englishman, with its stockade and tall proud bastions. Lately the fort is buzzing with gold talk, as trappers and Indians bring in nuggets along with their pelts, and there's a strange excitement in the air. But it's calm at home here in the shack. It smelled richly of cedar once, but that left long ago.

There is an uneven chest of drawers against the wall, with a bent-box on top, dusty, empty — or maybe it holds something. It belonged to Rose. Her Indian grandfather made it for her by hand, patiently, without nails. A copper kettle on the rough wood stove gathers sunshine on its curves, and blown dust settles like spilled salt on the floor's creaky boards.

The shack suits me well enough, time spinning its web through the cottonwood trees, the powerful surge of the Fraser forging its way to the sea, moonlight drenching the dark cedar boughs making night patterns through the window frame, wild things crying out in the dark, dawn when it arrives bringing the chatter of blue jays and crows fighting each other for the balls of fat I hang on the willow, and the pure joy of mornings with my daughter, Kami. Kalama I named her, for my mother in Honolulu.

In my mind's eye I see her now, my mother, picking papayas beside her grass hut. A simple tapa cloth is wrapped around her brown body. Not for her the prim missionary *muu-muu*. A white hibiscus blooms in her long black hair. She sways as she walks barefoot on the sand, head held high like a queen, and for a split second she's beside me and I can smell her mother scent, that mix of jasmine and plumeria from her skin, and she reaches for my hand. Then she laughs suddenly, as if she knows something I do not, and walks away and leaves me feeling like a lost child. And I look down and see my own child. It's dawn, and she stands beside me at the window. Every day she looks more like Rose, with her mother's eyes, straight nose and high Indian cheekbones. I've been neglecting her, I know, since her mother died. A pretty golden thing, she tugs at my heart. She points to the river. A flotilla of canoes is pushing out from the shore.

"Duck hunters," I say, unnecessarily.

"Can I go with Aunt Khatie?" She doesn't want to be with me. She wants to pick reeds and berries with the Kwantlen women and children, while the men are off at the hunt. She gazes up at me expec-

4

tantly, waiting for a word, for direction of some kind. From me, who can't even direct myself these days. And I think of the intuitive wisdom of children. The four-year-old knows more than I do. It's time to get about the business of life. For her sake. For my own.

"Yes, you can go," I say quickly, before I change my mind, and she laughs, an echo of her mother, and skips away. Last spring I buried Rose. I could recall the day in detail, but won't. I shut it out. Instantly. I've learned to do that. The past is dead. Done with, unalterable. My Hawaiian ancestors would mutilate themselves, break teeth or gouge out an eye over the death of a loved one, but even that would afford me no comfort, for there is no compensation for Rose's death. Resolve betrays me and it's her burial all over again. There she is, laid out like a broken doll that just needs mending. I breathe deeply, and mercifully the memory recedes. Time heals, they tell me. Meantime I've learned how to detach myself. I walk around like a whole man, but my heart's frozen. Hell is no place of fire after all but of cold nothingness. And anger — my right middle finger a crooked reminder of the day she died, when I smashed my fist into the wall.

Someone nearby starts whistling. It's Moku Mu'olelo. He's my *aikane*, my best friend. He picks up tunes from the boatmen at the fort, the voyageurs. In the Islands, we chanted songs and drummed before the whites, the *haolés*, brought European music and instruments. I can only manage bird calls and never made the leap to whistling songs, like Moku, who's come to ask if it's true I'm letting Kami go.

"Yes," I tell him. "If Khatie will take her."

"You can't guard her every minute of the day," he points out.

And don't I know that, I want to say, but don't. He means well. We're close as brothers, working as servants of the Hudson's Bay Company, which everybody knows is the nearest thing to God Almighty in this land. Moku's Kanaka, like me. He's open-hearted, a big man with brown eyes and shiny black hair that once rested on his

5

shoulders but is now cropped short around his ears. His nose is broad, his smile wide, exposing even white teeth. At six feet, he's an inch shorter than I, but broad and strong as an ox. Music is his passion and he finds any excuse to luau on Sunday afternoons till the sun goes down. I trust him like no other. It's his Kwantlen wife, Khatie, who looks after Kami while I work at the fort.

In the evenings, we weed and hoe our little plot of land beside the river. We staked it out together and took spades to dig up the big rectangle of wild grasses, salal and blackberry bushes. It took eight days to cut down two broad cedars, three alders and a giant cottonwood, leaving the stumps to rot. Moku calls it our "stump garden," and we work it between us, digging and hoeing the ground, composting leftover eggshells and food waste — though there's precious little waste, except for potato peelings. MacKay, the fort's Scottish scout, taught us to keep tea leaves and ashes from the stove to dig into the soil and to use leftover soap water from dishes and clothes to wash the bugs off the plants' leaves.

"Three bags today." Moku drops heavy woven reed bundles rattling with shells at his feet. We're building a sixteen-inch-wide pathway of crushed shells through the vegetable patch so the potatoes won't interfere with the onions, and the peas will have a place to reach for the sun, climbing up an army of stakes we're planting beside the path. Khatie gathers the clamshells from the beach during the day. Moku and I rake out the shells, stamp them with our boots into place, and stamp again, pleased with our work.

Moku nods at the city of tents sprung up beside the fort walls across the river. Hundreds of canvas triangles are pitched on the ground. The place has become a noisy way station, a holding area and tinder box of trouble for miners waiting for transport north to the goldfields.

"Every day more arrive," he says. "Daydreamers mostly, as if gold will fall into their laps, just like that. Did you ever see such an odd lot in your life? Men thin as straws, some fat as turkeys. Pencil-pushers, as well, who never laid hand or eye on a pick or shovel in their lives."

"But if a man were physically strong and used to hard work, he might have an advantage. If he had a goal in mind. If he wanted money for a particular reason," I say.

Moku rests his brown arms on the shovel. "What kind of reason?"

"It's risky, but it could be a fast way to raise money. To buy land, or pay your family's way back to Hawaii, for instance. We'll be dead before we save enough from what the Company pays us." I'm thinking now of the Hudson's Bay Company and its proud flag with the bold black H.B.C. initials emblazoned on the front. Between themselves, men whisper the initials stand for *Here Before Christ*, for it seems the Company's grip on the land will never end. Free traders are weary waiting for it to happen. But the Company's been fair enough to me. I wouldn't have stayed otherwise. Still, there was a time when I thought of leaving to join the free traders, to make money enough to buy land of my own. I'm not sure when that dream faded, and the daily routine of living just took over.

"Supposing all this gold talk is exaggerated?" Moku says. "And the Californians are up here chasing an empty dream, now their own gold rush is over?"

"It's been assayed," I remind him. "It's real. And they're not all Californians. They're from England, France, Germany, all over."

"You're not planning to join them, are you?" he says.

"How can I? I just signed a new contract." But the reason I left Hawaii in the first place was to earn money to buy land at the end of my three-year stint with the Company. My plan was to go back, but then I married Rose and stayed, and as the years rolled by, I had no notion to return, for here we lived content. We had each other and Kami came along, after ten years, when we'd almost given up hope.

But now the notion has come back. To own land, be independent — to live freely, grow food, raise chickens or a pig or two, and know your child won't go hungry. Either here, after *Here Before Christ* gives up control, which rumour says will come soon, or maybe back in Honolulu at the end of my contract, for I'm thinking more and more about the Islands these days. Either way, money's the key.

Memories of Rose rush at me now, but I resist fiercely and turn my attention back to Moku. It's been seventeen years since we sailed together from Honolulu to Fort Vancouver on the Columbia River. We'd signed a contract in the Hudson's Bay recruiting office, a wooden shack on the docks of Honolulu, to work for the Company in their forts on the Pacific Northwest Coast of America. On arrival, they sent us north to the Langley fort. We signed up for three years, but Moku married Khatie, a native Kwantlen woman and I married Rose, half white, half native, and we stayed. Moku has two grown daughters now, married at thirteen and fourteen, as Indian women do. Keiki, their son, arrived later. He's five, the image of his father, and a playmate for my Kami, who follows him around like a puppy.

"Californians, Europeans, whoever they are," Moku says of the miners camping at the fort, "they bring no end of trouble. They should've stayed home where they belong. Which is where I'm heading right now."

And that's the end of our conversation because he lifts his shovel and heads for home, whistling. That works for Moku, but not for me, for I'm not sure where home is any more. Rose was home, but she's dead. And the opportunity for independence, for the chance to buy land here hasn't happened yet. The Company still controls everything. The free traders insist change is coming soon, but they've been saying that for years. We had dreams, Rose and I, but somehow, we let them drift. My wage never did stretch far, but I think now that contentment blinded us into not looking ahead. I blame myself. But opportunity's come knocking now, for men are finding gold along the Fraser. I've seen the yellow nuggets with my own eyes. But for me now, the timing's wrong. My contract is for five years.

At bedtime, Kami sleeps soundly. It's a mystery dear to me, a mystery I thank my lucky stars for, that this child was born to us after so long. As long as I have her, I have a part of Rose. She comes to me at night, Rose does, for the dead can walk in dreams. But this night is different, for when I sleep, my dreams carry me far from the wrinkled grey of the Fraser and the bearded miners camping at the fort, across the blue Pacific to Honolulu and the grass shack where I was born. I can smell the burnt grass scent of the ti-leaf mat covering the red dirt floor, and the fragrant frangipani beside the lanai, with its drooping leaves. I split a coconut with a single blow from my grandfather's machete, feel its milk dribble down my chin, and relish the trade wind breeze kissing my warm skin. This is the long-ago time of my life, when my mother sings songs and dances the hula, before my father dies of the pox, and I sit on the tapa mat laughing, laughing with them, laughing joyously, amazed at my good fortune. Things are simple. The world is easy. The ocean waves shush softly up the warm sand and voices shimmer on the wind as night falls and begins its slow drift through the swaying branches of the palms.

chapter two

I RISE EARLY, FEED Kami, and walk with her to Moku's shack near where the little creek enters the river. The running water has a name, Kanaka Creek. Single men and white men with Indian wives live inside the fort, and voyageurs with wives too, but Hawaiians with Indian wives live outside, here at the creek on the north side of the Fraser, and on other parts of the river. We live content among ourselves, holding to Island ways while learning those of the Europeans and the native people. It's a challenge that defeats many, but with Rose I found my fit in this wild place. Without her, the fit no longer sits well, like a collar grown too tight.

Each morning, I paddle with Moku and Como, the fort's aging cook, across the river to the fort. Usually in silence. The old man wastes few words. His head is a dome of white stubble, and though his back is bent, his muscles are still powerful and he paddles well.

The work bell rings at 6 a.m. sharp and we're never late. Today, the river is racing. It's late April and the water's a surging, silt-laden mass, high and grey-brown, not its usual blue or green. We respect the Fraser's moods and concentrate in silence, coordinating our strokes. You don't take this river for granted, even its lower reaches. We reach the dock, climb out, haul the canoe up and turn it over. We tie it securely, then head up to the fort.

We wend our way through the sprawl of tents around the stockade walls, row after row, all the way from the river's edge. Some are single canvas covers, others accommodate groups of four or more. The air reeks of bacon, beans and bannock, of leathers and sweat and of tobacco being smoked. A few men sleep; others have been up all night. Some are busy already, shaving in front of tent flaps and cooking food in pots on tripods suspended over small wood fires. Others are gambling, even at this time of the morning, throwing dice on makeshift boards or playing cards for English pennies and American dollars.

There are rough, wild men here, of the sort to be avoided, but my body is well muscled from years of hard labour and I'm not worried. I judge them all simply as men — happy as dogs with a bone, sad as the bereaved, quiet as Mission men at prayer, or drunk as lords, riotous with camaraderie or lonesome as the desert pine, a ragtag bunch of human beings rigging up semblances of home, compelled to create a world for themselves, even if it's only under soiled sheets of canvas.

They've come from Victoria. Hundreds arrive there every day from San Francisco. They make their way across the Georgia Strait to the mouth of the Fraser and thirty miles upriver to Langley, for the journey north to the goldfields. Countless men have drowned before they reach the mainland in the Strait's treacherous riptides. But undaunted, they come.

"It'll get worse," predicts Moku, who picks up information from the clerks. They speak freely in front of him, so preoccupied are they with the problems created by the influx of miners. The numbers are astonishing.

"A ship landed nineteen hundred last week, though they say its record lists half that many," Como says. "They fake the numbers. Hundreds aren't accounted for. Men in San Francisco who can't afford a steamer pay to sail up in rotten hulks, death traps patched with putty. And still they keep pouring in."

"And what's the Company doing about it?" Moku wants to know. "If any more Californians arrive on our doorstep, it'll be a madhouse. They won't even recognize the border, for heaven's sake."

He's right. They're a rambunctious lot. The boundary dispute was settled at the 49th parallel in 1846 by the Treaty of Oregon and, considering Britain lost the Oregon Territory, the Americans' ongoing peevishness makes no sense.

"They still figure it's their destiny to rule the continent and they're mad as hell when Victoria tries to enforce British law. They actually believe rules don't apply to them."

It's true. They're impatient and aggressive to a degree that shocks the local people, whites and Indians alike.

"Victoria won't let things get out of hand," Como assures us, though I'm not so sure the tide of freewheeling Americans can be controlled by the staid British. More fights have broken out in the last two weeks than in all the years I've worked at the fort. And it comes to me, that's near enough twenty years, and I feel a queer twist in the pit of my stomach. Not regret for coming, no — but something sad all the same and a sense of loss. It swamps you at times, the sense of loss. And it comes screaming at me now before I can stop it, like an arrow piercing the heart, that I've lost the love of my life, and I myself am wandering lost in a sad place. But wandering's the wrong word, so I peck about in my Hawaiian brain till the right English word comes. Outcast. That's it. A wanderer can travel here and there and whistle in the wind if he takes the notion. But an outcast is alone in a strange place, with nowhere to go.

"The trouble is, they're all packing guns." Moku's peeved. He has a passion for guns himself. He dreams of owning a "Thumbbuster" like the Americans are carrying. It's the new Colt Single Action .44 or .45, with a four and three-quarter-inch barrel and black rubber grips. You cock it by pulling the hammer back before firing, using the second joint of the thumb, not the ball of your thumb. If you're careless, you can give yourself a busted thumb for your efforts — and sometimes shoot yourself in the foot.

"And one pistol's never enough. No, they tote a pair and strut about with rifles as well, if they can manage. Not to mention Bowie knives." Which rattles the conservative British no end. And this all because our fort sent the gold brought in by the Indians to the closest mint for assay — San Francisco. Word leaked out, and American miners rushed to the Fraser and discovered gold outside of Hope. Hill's Bar triggered a stampede and the fort clerks in Langley and Victoria have been struggling since to cope with the demands made by many hundreds of men arriving on their doorstep needing to be fed, housed and supplied with the tools and necessities for a trip to the goldfields.

Among the camping miners is a Negraman, the first I've seen, though men say there are others in the tents. I've never known a man so tall, with a face black as lava and skin shining like polished ebony, a great white smile cracking his face like a tear in cloth, and a gap between his front teeth you could drive a cart through. He is alone, with no partner in his tent, and nods a polite *Mawnin'*, as we go by.

I look for him each day, though I never need to look hard, for the man stands out like a lone cedar in a stump meadow. I told Kami about the black man when I got home, for he astonished me as much as my first encounter with a Chinaman — bald but for the single black braid down his back — that I saw unloading tea casks on the docks in Honolulu.

Every day there's trouble in the tents, with brawling miners pulling knives, and it's no surprise when another fight breaks out as we're heading home after a day's work at the fort. We're forced to an abrupt halt as two men surge into our path, circling each other with knives in hand. I crane my neck for a closer look. Something about the tall man catches my eye. Scars criss-cross his cheeks from knife cuts and the pox. Long black hair, unwashed and limp, cascades to his shoulders and one of his dark eyes is crusted with infection. He spits at his opponent and curses, and suddenly I recognize the deep Hawaiian voice. Age has weathered his face, and he's lost weight, but it's the Kanaka Ahuhu. There's no doubt.

"Shit!" Moku says, because I've already stepped forward when he grabs for my arm to hold me back, but I shake him off. And I'm in the midst of the fight before he can stop me.

"Drop the knife, Ahuhu!" I bark. How could he be such a fool, camping this close to a Company fort, instigating a fight and drawing attention to himself? "Lay down that blade!" I step between the two men. Bile rises in my throat. Just speaking his name has fetched up the bad taste. *Ahuhu* means poison weed in Hawaiian. It's a name he chose for himself, for some perverse reason. Men leaving the Islands one step ahead of the law do that sometimes, change their name.

He starts coughing so hard, his knife hand shakes. "Stay out of this, Kanui!" he warns, waving his blade at me while still circling his opponent, a bow-legged little man, thin as a rail, with strings of fair hair topping a bald head. The little man's face is the colour of putty, and from each side of his nose, two thin blue slits stare out. He hunches over, inching his way backwards when the Kanaka lunges, making him stumble and pitch to the ground where he sprawls on his back.

"The bastard stole my gear," the little man sputters. He sounds English and is outraged, but his squeaky nasal voice holds no authority, and Ahuhu laughs at him.

"End this now, Ahuhu, or I'll see you clapped in irons." I clench my teeth; it's so hard to keep control. He's a runaway from Fort Vancouver. Years ago he tried to kill Rose and her family. He'd bargained for her, to use and abuse, knowing he had the "Chinook Love Fever" or gonorrhea. Last I saw him by Semiahmoo Bay, he was roving with a band of thieves and fort runaways. "There's a jail cell waiting for you," I remind him.

"You wouldn't do that to a fellow Kanaka," he jeers with the cold truth of a scalpel.

He's right. I hate him knowing me so well. I wouldn't hand any man over to the Company. They punish harshly for breaking rules, clamping men in irons and chaining them like animals for months. Yet if anyone deserves such cruelty, it's Ahuhu. Fifteen years ago I nearly beat him to death, and his sudden appearance brings it back. A great wave of hate surges through me. I'm itching to use the knife stowed in my belt and I want him to make a move, now, more than anything in the world.

"Try me!" I say, but he reads the rage in my eyes, lowers his blade and steps back.

Moku helps me hoist the Englishman to his feet. We're still lifting him under the armpits when Ahuhu darts forward, arm raised, blade clutched in his fingers. He comes at me, aiming the knife at my chest, when the big Negraman suddenly steps out from the crowd and strikes Ahuhu's arm sharply with a downward drop of his own big arm. The blade falls harmlessly to the ground and the black man hoists Ahuhu up in the air by his shirt collar.

"He gwan git you with that blade, Kanaka," he says, shaking Ahuhu from side to side like wet laundry. Then he lowers him slowly, inch by inch, till Ahuhu's feet touch the ground, but grips him still around the collar like a choked dog. I clench my fists. So often this past year I've wanted to beat something, or somebody, out of sheer frustration and misery and I've every reason now to smash Ahuhu into pulp. I take over from the Negraman, and grip Ahuhu by the front of his soiled shirt and pull him close, eye to eye, nose to nose. I'm shaking from want of throttling him. But I hold back and breathe deeply. It's vengeance I'm after, not just for the man's cruelty years ago and the cut he meant to deliver today, but for the hell my life has been since Rose died. And Ahuhu is not responsible for that.

"Your luck's used up," I tell him. "Men here won't put up with thieving. If I set eyes on you again, you're dead. *Pau!* Finished. Hear me?"

His wet spittle spatters my cheek, and I hit him hard, for a man must answer such an insult. Then I rap the side of my hand sharply across his throat and he doubles over choking.

"Get out of my sight. Now, if you know what's good for you before the smith hammers chains on you. Or I'll do it myself, just for the pleasure. Move!" I release him with a shove, making him stumble backwards. He curses and takes off at a half trot through the tents. He brings shame to the name Kanaka.

"We're not done, Kanui!"

There's fury in his voice, but I turn my back on his ravings. The man is sick, one cough short of a coffin. I should feel sorry for him. I don't.

I want to thank the Negraman, but he's disappeared. Later, I find him at his tent, squatting on his haunches in front of a wooden block, with a mouthful of tacks. His hands are full, one with a hammer, the other holding the sole of a boot the size of a bucket. The boot sits on a makeshift last, a rectangular metal block. He's attaching a piece of rough cut leather to the worn-out sole, and spits out a tack. His big fingers seize it and in the blink of an eye he's hammered it into place at the edge.

"Thanks for your help." I extend my hand. He lays the hammer down and tacks come shooting from his mouth, sparkling like tiny shooting stars, one after the other into his palm, and he sets them down beside the hammer. He's slow to shake hands, but then one big black hand reaches out, and my not-small-fist feels caught like a nut in a grinder.

"That's aw'right, suh," he says. "The man's a thief. Folks all know he stole more'n enough around this place."

In the days and weeks that follow, I stop at the black man's tent on my way to work. His name is Ezekiel Jeremiah Browne and he was born in North Carolina. He speaks slowly, deliberately, as if pondering every word before he lets it fall from his mouth. He says slaves are being freed in some states in America, but black men are still dying in the south and it looks like there's no stopping it soon. He left Carolina "a whiles back," he says, and moved to California, where he worked doing odd jobs and mining. But I wonder where a slave, even a freed one, would find the money to move from Carolina to California, and then to Victoria and Langley, and I sense there's some mystery to this big man. He says he's come to try his luck in the goldfields. Other blacks have run from the slave states to this northern country to find freedom, and to avoid the trouble that's brewing over slavery in their own land. The Negraman thinks slavery doesn't exist here.

"It still does, in places," I tell him, "among the natives. Though they don't sell or barter people so much now, not since the Catholic priest arrived. The river tribes flocked to hear his sermons and converted in droves. They were glad to be rid of slavery and their old caste systems. But still, it happens."

18

I remember the priest coming the year the fort burned down, because Rose converted then. Her father Jacques had taught her the basics of the Catholic faith, so she was eager to attend Father Demers' sermons outside the fort. I went once or twice, for I'd attended the Mission in Honolulu and learned Christianity. But truth to tell, there are days I sense the old Hawaiian gods speak to me still, though their voices have grown weak in this cold land. Rose, though, found strength in her faith. That's why I gave her a Christian burial. Her Kwantlen family wanted her treed, native style — bundled and placed on a platform high in a cedar, away from wolves and bears and things that forage in the night. I push the memory away. I must, or I won't function. My insides are already knotting in a cold hard ball.

I leave Ezekiel and wend my way through the camp. You could cut the air with a knife in this tent city. The four hundred men camped by the fort give off a smell now, but there's an air of something else as well, something indefinable. They've got properly dug latrines, the fort insists on that, but it's not the animal smells that my senses pick up. It's other things. Naked greed for one. It's easy to recognize. It emanates off certain individuals. More importantly though, and unrelated to financial gain, there's an atmosphere charged with the exhilaration of challenge, physical and mental, an excitement and sort of bravado among the men. And it's contagious, as if some giant organism has run amok, swarming and spreading infection, one that defies reality, for each man is convinced bad luck may well strike another but not himself, that he is somehow immune. Men feed off each other, and excitement builds.

I feel it myself. The notion has been creeping up on me that I too should seek my fortune in the goldfields. But I just renewed my contract with the Company and I won't break it. So there'll be no part in the Fraser gold rush for me.

But still the idea returns to rise from time to time, like fish on a line, defying logic. I concoct scenarios in my head as if it were a real possibility. If I were to go, my worry would be Kami. Khatie would take her, but the child might feel abandoned. She's already lost her mother. So I reject the idea again, and go work the garden each evening with Moku, and hammer squared cedar posts into the ground to support the vines. Moku's been working in the fort's trade store lately, where the lineup of men buying supplies is endless.

"There's no keeping up with their demands. We've run out of shovels, flour and soap, and they complain we charge more than Victoria."

"The day won't dawn that the Company doesn't make money. They must be pleased enough with the profits they rake in."

"Nothing's cheap," Moku says. "Tobacco's $6.00. Flour $1.50 a pound, pork and beef $1.00 a pound, beans $1.45. You need supplies for three or more months. Add a gun. And a strong canoe. And poles and rope for hauling the canoe along tough stretches of the river. You need a heap of money before you can even begin to look for gold."

"Money's not the big worry. It's the river. Where it's too wild, men leave it and walk the bank in teams, hauling their canoes along with ropes. MacKay says they do that in Europe, with horses towing barges along canals. Only here it's men doing the towing. But the canyon? No. Even the Indians won't try it. They go up and over it. MacKay tried canoeing it once and nearly died. The Indians brought him through, along the steep cuts by the river's edge, hauling themselves up one after the other with the use of long poles, and then up over the mountain top and around the river."

"*Ae.* Yes. He went through hell climbing the canyon," Moku says. "Yet some fools think they can do it . . . loaded with heavy packs and all." It's true. We hear of miners toting packs trying to traverse the canyon's precipices, but notches cut into the mountainsides by Indians don't work for heavy leather boots and men keep falling into the river and drowning. "They just don't know what they're up against."

The trouble is, most men have never seen a river with power like the Fraser. It flows eight hundred miles to the sea, through the high Rocky Mountains where snow can lie feet deep for ten months of the year and longer. You can find your way around the delta, as the river slows and opens wide, but a hundred miles inland, it slices its way through the Coast Mountains and charges through the canyon — Hell's Gate, men have begun calling it — at terrifying speeds impossible to navigate.

"There's no arguing the river route is swallowing up men," I say, "but if a man planned well, calculated the risks beforehand and determined not to be reckless, there's a good chance he'd succeed."

"It's too dangerous," Moku insists, and starts whistling a jig, some tune MacKay plays on his pipes. I stop tying up the vines and wait for him to finish hoeing the row of potatoes. There's no point in talking further when Moku's in this mood. Besides, he's right. And that should be the end of it for a man of good sense, so I say no more about it and neither does he, and we work the loamy soil till dusk. I'm under contract and not free to do other than I'm doing anyway, and that's the way of it, so I follow my routine and work hard each day, because that's how I am. Still, I listen to every bit of news that comes in of events in the goldfields and gather information.

It costs twenty-two shillings, or five dollars for a mining licence. Gold is heavier than anything else found with it, and has a specific gravity of nineteen, compared to regular sand which reads two or three, or black sand that reads about five. Specific gravity refers to the displacement of gold, the measure of its sinkability, for gold is always found at the bottom of the pan. Panning is slow, hard work. A rocker is better because it is mobile, and a sluice box is best of all because it can handle larger loads of gravel. But you must channel water into a sluice box, and this can be difficult. Still, the process doesn't sound too complex, and I don't think it requires an overdose of brain power. When I see the types of men heading for the gold-fields, I think I could do as well. If I were free to go — which of course I'm not.

I regret having signed again. Habit, I suppose. I just did it because that's what I've always done. Who could have known there would be so much gold on the Fraser? But now I'm ready for change. I still miss Rose. I expect I always will. Time dulls the edge of grief but it has a way of coming back when you least expect it. But it's more than grief eating at me now. I'm no longer the man I was. I'm unsettled, discontented with this place, with my work, with my life. And I've begun to think of the warm islands I left behind. But thank good-ness, Kami seems content. I spend all my free time with her, feeling no inclination to drink or gamble with the fort's men. I'm raising my child alone, as my mother did me. With the help of *ohana*, Rose's parents.

Neetlum and Lawiq'um visit our shack on Sunday afternoons, the only time I have off work. They come to see their granddaughter, and miss only when they portage south to meet relatives at Semiahmoo Bay in the spring and fall. Neetlum's love for Kami surprises me, since Rose was not his child. Lawiq'um married the voyageur, Jacques Fanon, who fathered Rose. When Jacques abandoned his family, Lawiq'um then married Neetlum, who never wanted Rose to marry me, a Kanaka, low in the fort's hierarchy, but he has come around with the passage of time and we approach each other now with mu-tual respect. He dotes on Kami, indulging her in a way he never did his own children, as my Hawaiian *kupuna*, my grandfather, indulged me too, which is perhaps the way of things.

They're late. Indians are lax about time. They come when it suits, and go when it suits, and it's never the same, so I stay with my carving. I'm making a halibut hook, working on the mold that will hold the steamed wood, concentrating so hard I don't hear the shout. But then I do, and it's Lawiq'um calling me, her voice so high and reedy I have trouble recognizing it. My wife's mother comes stumbling along the dirt path, ashen-faced, almond eyes aglitter with fright.

"What's wrong? Where's Neetlum?"

"By the river's edge," she pants. "Quick! He needs help."

I rush off, and shout as I pass Moku's door, and he's suddenly with me, racing to the riverbank. Neetlum is there, and I breathe a sigh of relief. My first thought was the old man had been felled by a heart attack, or had his foot caught in a trap, but the Kwantlen is fine. Except for the look on his face. He is struggling to haul something out of the water. At first, I think it's a log, then a bundle of rags.

"It's a man," Moku says.

We swallow hard. It's one thing to pull a dead man from the river; it's another when he's hacked to pieces and has the scalp torn off his head. We haul the lifeless mass up the muddy river bank.

"What kind of man is he?" the old Indian asks, and it's not so odd a question. Not long ago, any man here would be native. But now he could be anything. We turn him over.

"*Haolé*," Moku says in Hawaiian, meaning white. "Hard to tell, the mess he's in."

"*Xwelitem*," Neetlum agrees, in Halq'emeylem.

"A miner, I reckon. We should notify the fort." I turn away. I can hardly bear to look at the man, what's left of him.

"I'll go," Moku says, and off he runs at a lope for the canoe. He clambers in and paddles across the river to Fort Langley as fast as his big arms can pull him while I squat on my haunches beside Neetlum. His shoulder-length hair, oiled black in his younger days, is tied back in a knot of thin grey wisps. His almond eyes are closed and I read weariness in his lined face.

"It's begun," he sighs. "Trouble now."

So I know this will be the first but not the only body to wash up on the muddy banks of the Fraser. We squat beside the body. Our nostrils quiver from the stink.

"No boots," Neetlum grunts.

I turn the bundle over. "No guns, no knife either. They've stripped him."

"The tribes are on the warpath," he says.

It's been rumoured for weeks. "Which ones, Neetlum?"

"Maybe all, north of Fort Yale."

We fall silent, each with his own thoughts, till Moku returns with one of the voyageurs and the Scot, MacKay. MacKay kneels and turns the body over and covers the corpse with a thin grey blanket from his pack.

"Well," he says, "that's it. The fighting's started."

The poor soul washed up today is proof of that, with his body mutilated beyond recognition, and his scalp peeled back like skin off an onion. MacKay goes through the man's pockets for identification but finds none and asks me for a shovel. We don't want to dump his body in the river, nor bury him near the riverbank, so we trudge through Kanaka Creek village, past the shacks. The children are rushed indoors by their mothers, and men stand in the doorways in silence. We walk into the brush beyond the village, carrying the body in the blanket, a man at each of its four corners. We dig a trench, and it takes awhile, though Moku goes back to retrieve another shovel. We roll the man in the blanket and lay him in the ground and shovel the cold dirt over him. It's a sad ending for a man, to die such a way and be buried such a way, but we do our best. MacKay says a prayer over the grave, marking it with a small pile of stones, a cairn, he calls it. He says it's a custom in his land. And we return to the village, and to our own thoughts.

I sit with Neetlum on my shack's wooden steps. Moku fetches a bottle from his house and fills three tin cups. In the fort's early days, men could only get rum, but now whiskey is the preferred drink of Indian and white alike. The *tanglelegs* steadies us.

"When this killing gets out, it'll slow down the stampede," Moku says.

Neetlum fills his pipe, lights it with fort matches, and draws the smoke into his lungs. "War is like disease; it spreads. The tribes are angry. They think the gold belongs to them. It's our land. But the miners want to take it all, not even to share it. This is a bad thing. And it's not only the gold. The Americans treat my people badly. They bring their war against the Indians up here and have no respect. And they take our women for wives."

"The tribes have reason to be angry," I agree, for I feel sorry over the disrespect and stealing of wives and it's right they'd want to do something about it. Though still, I wonder if it's not the wish for gold that's truly brought on the killings, for greed will do that to men. "But butchering people, hacking them to bits and mutilating them is no answer."

I can't stop thinking about the nameless man we just buried. Who was he? Where did he come from? What life did he envision for himself? Had he a wife or child, I wonder? Did he go to the goldfields with their blessing, or was it his own dream he followed? No matter. He's six feet under the cold earth now, a man with no name.

And I wonder what the hard-headed Californians will do now, faced with tribal warfare along the Fraser? Will they heed the warning and turn back, or press ahead regardless? How many nameless men will need burying? As for my own fascination with the goldfields lately, I'll forget about that. For if more men need to be buried in the search for gold, I prefer to be at the living end of the shovel.

chapter three

News of the Indian uprising doesn't deter the miners one whit. Month after month they keep arriving in Langley and keep leaving for the goldfields. Nothing but nothing stops them. We hear rumours of one strike after another, of gold lying on the surface of the ground, in places jutting out for the picking. Of men finding $25, even $75, in one pan. Men who never heard the words before are discussing the merits of rockers and sluice boxes.

"American seamen are deserting their ships for the goldfields," Moku reports that night, while we're working the garden.

"Yes. And soldiers from Fort Douglas and Bellingham are deserting their posts as well." Many are doing it, voyageurs and Kanakas too, running from the Company mid-contract to join the gold-seekers. "Deserters and runaways, they'll be the ones that turn back early, that don't stay the course," I tell him, because in my mind men who flee obligations are weak. A man runs once, he'll likely run again in the face of adversity. From what I've heard, in the goldfields, rashness of nature will get you killed. But I feel sorry for them all the same, for gold has the power to draw men, inexplicably, like moths to flame. And logic seems to have no part in it.

So many go rashly, unprepared, that nine out of ten are turning back. No one knows how many are dying in the winter cold, in the rivers and mountains and valleys, or at the hands of the Indians. Most miners are still taking the original canyon route, Hope to Yale, to the forks at Lytton and beyond, and the Fraser still floats butchered bodies downstream. Neetlum tells us the war is retaliation for a young Nlaka'pamux woman being raped by some miners. Then we hear at the fort that prospectors from the Fraser and Thompson have retreated to Spuzzum and Yale, that some are caught at China Bar, where twenty-one of them are killed by Indians picking them off one by one. Only four survive. Another is injured with seven arrows in him.

Then, good news. The government sends volunteer troops from Yale. Before they even arrive, a truce has been brought about by Cam-chin chief Cxpentlum of the Nlaka'pamux, and his allies the Secwe-pemc and the Okanagan Indians. Whether the wise chief truly wished for peace, or knew the troops were on their way, the outcome results in peace treaties being signed with all six tribes between Yale and Lytton. With the war over, miners biding their time in Yale return to stake claims 200 miles along the Fraser. Yet even as thousands head upriver, men by the hundreds are coming down, beaten by the dreadful hardships of the land, as well as from sickness or wounds from the Indian wars.

Moku has news of the diggings. At the store, he hears things: that men are pressing farther up the Fraser on and out along the river's many small rivers and creeks; that another two hundred men arrived at the fort today. "Douglas set a gunboat at the mouth of the Fraser to collect licences from miners trying to make their way upstream without going through Victoria."

"They're fools to think they can get anything by James Douglas," I say, though I don't doubt many will try. Douglas is the Company's big *kahuna*, the main chief, here on the coast. He's a big man, strong, with rock-like features and bold eyes that peer out under a shelf of dark eyebrows, with a true air of authority about him. In Hawaii, he'd make a worthy chief, a *moi*. There a chief must be physically large and powerful to rule. Here I learned otherwise.

It troubled me when I first arrived that our chief clerk Yale was so little, but the man's spirit belies his size. He has tenacity and courage. We battled the natives here in the early days, as well as fire and floods, and Little Yale stands tall as any man I know — except for Douglas, who wears two hats, minding the Company's interests while acting as Governor of Vancouver Island.

The Company moved headquarters from Fort Vancouver on the Columbia River to Fort Victoria during the border dispute, and the Gulf Islands and Vancouver Island became a crown colony in 1849, with Douglas as governor. Now, nine years later, the mainland too is becoming a crown colony; we are no longer to be New Caledonia, but British Columbia.

What a day it is. Never before have there been so many *kahunas* in our fort, all come up on the steamer *Beaver* to Langley for the ceremony. The ship pounds out an 18-gun salute as the British flag rises above the fort. But in fact it flops drearily around the wet post because rain is sheeting down, and the ceremony has to move inside, to the upper room of the Big House. There Douglas appoints Matthew Baillie Begbie as Chief Justice of British Columbia, then Begbie appoints Douglas Governor of the Colony. I can't take my eyes off Begbie: a tall, lanky man, about 6'5", with white hair and a bushy black moustache. He's taller than any Englishman I've ever met, and speaks like one, though they say his parents are Scots. At the ceremony, Douglas delivers the proclamation revoking the right of exclusive privileges of the Hudson's Bay Company. At long last! Every free trader in the country will cheer the news!

Change happens so swiftly in this land that what anchors life keeps shifting. James Douglas has quit the Hudson's Bay to become Governor of British Columbia. I think of the whirlwind of change the whites brought to Hawaii, and I see the same hurricane winds blowing here. Only here the change is wilder. Miners with pistols are no missionaries with bibles.

Right away Douglas sets out to establish law and order through Judge Begbie, to curb the wild miners. Magistrates and constables arrive, along with 165 Royal Engineers — blacksmiths, surveyors, carpenters and others. Colonel Moody and his Engineers accompany Judge Begbie to Yale and Hill's Bar to settle trouble brewing there with the Americans come up through the Whatcom Trail illegally, defying British rules. Annexation by the Americans is a great fear around here. There are so many of them, especially Californians. They've done it before. They want to do it again. In the bars and saloons, miners are singing a song to the tune of Yankee Doodle:

> *Yankee Doodle wants a state,*
> *Oregon or Texas,*
> *Sends some squatters in it straight,*
> *And quietly annexes.*

But Judge Begbie quickly puts down the insurrection led by Ned McGowan and his American friends, and halts their efforts to overthrow British authority. The Engineers begin building roads and trails; there's excitement in the air and a sense of anticipation of great things to come. For me, it's like riding a great wave, cresting one of those giant Pacific rollers that tumbles headlong and crashes along Oahu's shore.

At the fort we hear that at the junction of the Fraser and Thompson, men are spading bars and benches and finding placer gold readily, for there's no bedrock and the yellow gold-bearing stratum is easily distinguished from the regular sand. New groups of men head north day after day, packing axes and optimism.

Geography has become the topic of all conversation. There's talk of the great watershed dividing the Cariboo, of gold-bearing rivers flowing into a great unnamed lake. Unknown rivers and streams are taking miners' names. The natives would argue that point. For thousands of years they've had names for them. But now places receive English names, as miners stake claims, hack their way through the wilderness, slash trees and build themselves log cabins. Miners have reached Fort Alexandria, Quesnelle Lake, Fort George. Americans find gold at Horsefly River. And more men rush north.

April rolls round again, the time of year when Moku and I busy ourselves working our garden, for the soil has warmed up enough to turn the ground over and plant vegetables, and the frosts can no longer kill.

"Contracts come up next month," he reminds me unnecessarily. Not ours though. We have two more years before they expire.

"We can expect the usual, then," I reply. At renewal time, men feel unsettled and want change, yet the foolish still fall for the Company ploy, drink too much of the free rum that just happens to be available for consumption around contract time, and wake up hung over in the morning signed up for another stint. Moku and I have always renewed, happy with our wives and families here and with our work with the Company. Though heaven knows, Kanakas could make more money working down south with the Americans, and this peeves us from time to time.

When my contract does expire, I have the option to re-sign, or to end it and remain here, or be returned.to Hawaii, passage paid. If I go back, I'll need to find the money for Kami's fare, for I won't go without her. Some men leave their native families behind when they go, often with not so much as a backward glance. The Company insists that families are provided for, but this usually amounts to the family being passed along to the next new man. Sometimes over and over. But I won't part with Kami. No. If I'm sure of nothing else, I'm sure of that. I daydream at times of crossing the sea with her, to live again under the hot Island sun, to run barefoot along the beach, feel warm sand work through my toes, while the cool trade wind blows overhead and people loll beneath the shade of the waving palms. With money, I could make it happen. With money from the goldfields.

The more I think of the goldfields, the stronger the urge to go. But I have to push the urge away. Time creeps by. My only compensation is watching Kami grow. Sometimes the urge to head north is fierce and strong when it blows through me, but I know so much is imagined, pictures concocted from stories and newspapers, some of them horrors, and I come to my senses. But it's not long before the urge blows back again, and I do believe it's worth chancing. Just not yet. Not until my obligation to the Company is over.

Moku complains now and again that he can never tell what I'm thinking, that I play my cards close to my chest. For some reason he admires this. He himself lacks prudence, and knows it. I wonder sometimes at our friendship. He respects my judgment and defers to me in many things, but I admire his quick mind, his determination, his plain, honest decency and see in him a better man than myself. I tell him what I'm thinking.

"When my contract expires, I won't renew."

He stops shovelling. "What will you do?"

"Try the goldfields."

"*Nah!* What do you know about sluice boxes and rockers or panning for gold? You couldn't tell gold from yellow rock!"

"A man can learn quick enough."

"It's too risky."

"Not if you plan well. Not if you're prepared."

"With the Indians above Yale killing miners still?"

"The Peace Treaty's holding up pretty good."

"They're still fighting in places."

"Neetlum trades regularly with the tribes up river," I counter. "Mostly you can avoid trouble if you don't go looking for it. Anyhow, I've still got to work out my time."

"Have you gone *lolo*? You're too old for a challenge like this."

"No. I'm not crazy, and forty's not so old." In fact, I'll be forty-two by then. "I can still handle myself in a fight, and I've lived long enough not to go looking for one."

"So your mind's made up?"

"It is, if Khatie will keep Kami till I get back."

"And how long will you be gone?"

"A few months. Depends on luck, and weather, and whatever else might crop up. If I find gold — and my chances are as good as the next man's — when I get enough, I'll buy myself a plot of land. Maybe even back in Oahu, Moku. It's not the same for me here without Rose."

"Well, I wouldn't want to go back. Things must be different there now. You'll have time to change your mind, anyway. By the time your contract's up, the gold rush could well be over."

I hope he's wrong, for this will be my only chance to take Kami with me to Hawaii. I could never have taken Rose. Langley was her home, her life, where she fit. I couldn't take her from all that. But I can take my child. With money from the goldfields. And it will feel good to be among my own people again, to belong, to feel equal.

I've never lost much sleep over the issue of prejudice here at the fort, but there's no denying it's a fact. You're judged by your skin colour, not your abilities. Most Kanakas working for the Company are illiterate, it's true. Our history was oral, and our written alphabet only recent and simple, worked out by the missionaries — seven consonants, H, K, L, M, N, P, W, and five vowels, A, E, I, O and U. I learned to read and write English at the Mission but it means nothing here. I'll never be a clerk. I'm viewed only as a workhorse, below the social and pay scale of white Europeans or the Canadiens or other mixed whites, though supposedly above the natives, who have taught us so much about living in this land. I have great respect for Mr. Douglas, but it surprises me being half white himself, and with a native wife, that skin colour affects fort policy to the degree it does. Of course, his orders come from London, from frock-coated gentlemen who know nothing about life here. If I didn't know my own worth as a man, the fort's hierarchy could offend me more than it does. I wonder what my grandfather would think. A warrior in the days when the fury of war gripped our Islands, my *kupuna* was a man of great stature. People looked up to him. He wanted so much more for me, sending me to the Mission to learn English and the *haolé* ways. Hah! Yet here I am. So there are many days I think Kami and I might have a better life among my own people.

Still, maybe Moku's right. There must be great changes in Hawaii since we left. I didn't resent the *haolés* coming, as many did, for the good old days in Hawaii were anything but good. The *alii*, the elite, held all the wealth, all the land, while the people were slaves. When I left, the Islands were in turmoil. Ancient systems were breaking down and new ones rising. Change brought upheaval and pain. I just hope the *haolés* have wrought more good than bad. Nothing can alter the fact they've rooted themselves now into Hawaii's rich soil, for good or ill. Still, as far as my worth as a man goes, I think I'd find more acceptance there than here in Langley.

At the fort, things keep changing. Mr. Yale leaves and I'm sad to see him go. William Newton becomes clerk for a few months before George Blenkinsop takes over as chief trader. After a few more months, Mr. Newton's back in charge. But I miss Yale and his infallible orders. Governor Douglas wanted the town site of Derby to be the new colony's capital, but Colonel Moody decides its location is too open to attack by the Americans. So instead, New Westminster, old Queensborough, becomes the new capital.

A new missionary, William Crickmer, arrives and sets up services in the engineer's barracks at Derby, preaching sometimes from a barrel on Main Street till they build a church for him, St. John the Divine. I wonder what he thinks about his flock perched in their pews on Sundays, decked out with Colts and Bowie knives.

In this whirlwind of change, with the *Here Before Christ* rule over the land finally over, the colony gets down to setting out rules for individuals to own land. I expect the Company's big *kahunas* must feel sick about all this, for it's a powerful loss. But it's the opportunity ordinary men have been waiting for.

"The Victoria newspaper says land can be pre-empted," I tell Moku. Though I don't know how it works in detail. I pass news from the papers to Moku, because he can't read or write. I don't think he felt any need for it before, but lately he's come to think it might be a good thing. I've offered to teach him, so one of these days, we'll need to start.

"What's pre-empted?" he asks.

"It means you can acquire it from the government at a discount price, or at no charge, providing you make certain improvements to it."

"That can't be hard," Moku says. "Clear some trees, build a shack, move some chickens or pigs on to the property. That would be called improving the land, right? Sounds good to me."

"You can also buy land from the government outright or through auction, for ten shillings an acre, half cash, with the balance in two years. It sounds good all right, but a man would still need to have money even for this. You're not earning while you clear the land, so you must have savings enough to survive the weeks and months of toil improving it. And money to buy chickens or pigs or cattle, or whatever stock you choose to raise on the property. And for the seed for planting."

Some have the means though, for it's happening around Victoria. And here, too, a man named Morrison has taken up 160 acres just upriver from the fort. One John McIver also takes up land west of the fort, though there's talk some of it is Q'eyts'i land, so he may have to move. All this keeps me awake at night thinking. Taking up land here is possible for the first time, right here, right now. There's something empowering about owning your own piece of the earth. I can almost feel the clumps of crumbled brown dirt dribbling through my fingers. The freedom, the pride, that simple dirt can give a man. You just need to stake out the four corners of the land you choose, and pay a registration fee of eight shillings to the nearest magistrate. James Houston's done it, come back to Langley after making a fortune in the gold-fields, to farm along the Salmon River. He's built a house, cleared the land, driven up cattle from Oregon, and now he's married a Nanaimo native woman converted to Christianity by Thomas Crosby, the Methodist missionary working there. But it all takes money to set up and make it work.

The wilderness around our fort is now a sea of shops and businesses and people. All kinds of people. You can buy bacon and eggs for breakfast from Hi Sing's shop on Main Street from a Chinaman wearing pigtails. The change is exhilarating. You feel swept up in it. And sometimes drowned by it.

Nothing changes for me though, as I continue to work out the remainder of my contract, but it's hard work. I'm impatient, but do what I must. I won't break my contract. A man's word must be worth something so I bide my time. Fort work has always been hard but it varies so it's never boring. Some days I make kegs with the cooper, or mend tables and chairs or milk stools, for they're forever being broken. I cut staves, and help the boatmen make repairs. I'm a decent carpenter. Other days I work the fields, hoeing, planting potatoes, barley, peas. Sometimes it's working with the dairy cattle, and I don't mind that, for time seems to go faster when you work outdoors.

I make time at day's end to hang about the store for bits of news the miners bring to the fort. There was so much trouble at the canyon, men have been opting for the lake route to the Cariboo, following the Fraser and Harrison rivers into Harrison Lake, to the new town of Port Douglas at the north end, then a portage over Harrison Trail to Lillooet Lake, then another portage to Anderson Lake, and into Cayoosh, now Lillooet.

It's a marvel to me how white men force nature and landscape to accommodate their wishes, for the new trail was barely begun through forest and rock and swamplands, and overnight commerce developed. And roadhouses are springing up every ten to fifteen miles apart for men to eat and rest and sleep overnight. I think the owners smart, mining the miners, finding another way to make money from the gold rush, rather than digging through hard rock with a shovel. And in the bustling new town of Port Douglas, at the north end of Harrison Lake, not much more than a long row of rough wooden shacks and tents, already there's a sawmill, and hotels and restaurants and stores. And it's the *haolé* way, I think, to plant a town like a bulb and have it spring instantly to life and spread itself across the landscape in the blink of an eye.

chapter four

WITH THE FRASER GOLD drying up, determined miners are trekking farther north — beyond the Fraser, creeping along the many creeks of the Cariboo, panning for gold and finding it. News gallops from tent to tent of the fortunes to be made. Gold is discovered at Little Horsefly Creek, then Doc Keithley and George Weaver find more at the headwaters of the Quesnelle River. It's so plentiful at Antler Creek — lying on the surface in places, they say — that you don't even need to dig for it. And so the rumours grow. Miners race north, oblivious of the season, and find they need to dig holes in the snow for shelter through the winter.

News of the gold strikes excites every man, myself included, and it's a strange twist of fate that the long delay turns out to be a good thing after all. Douglas has decided enough men have died in the canyon, that he's going to build a road to transfer men and goods safely to the northern goldfields. He begins with a wagon road to Spuzzum, then along the Fraser from Yale to Boston Bar, and from Lytton to Cook's Ferry on the Thompson River. The plan requires an extraordinary feat of engineering. But it's typical of the white man's mindset to think that obstacles exist to be overcome, so with implacable determination, the *haolés* proceed to impose their will on whatever stands in their way, geography be damned.

And so the Royal Engineers and civilian contractors do the impossible and in two years blast a passage four hundred miles through rocks and mountains and build a bridge across the river as well. It takes four hundred men. When many run off to the goldfields, the contractors replace them with Chinese and Indian labourers. The Indians are cut down by smallpox and the contractors fall behind, so Douglas sends engineers to finish the job. And before you know it, wagon trains weighing four thousand pounds apiece and hundreds of pack animals are on the road before it's even finished. It's the talk of every man heading for the Cariboo. And miners that the canyon repulsed prepare to try again.

"No Kanakas have come back, as far as I know, Moku. Our people likely handle the river better, being born to the paddle and used to wild water. We have an advantage."

"Ha! Wild water's one thing. Wild Indians are another," he retorts. But I've been mulling this over long enough, and if I'm going to go, now's the time. I missed the Fraser gold. I won't miss the Cariboo rush. Every Kanaka knows when you want to ride a wave, timing is everything. And now, at last, for me the time is right.

When I tell Kami that I'll be leaving for a while, she asks why, and I squat and hold her small hand and kiss her knuckles, and tell her I'm going to find gold to build her a fine house in a fine garden. She says we already have a fine house and a fine garden, and my throat catches, for her brown eyes remind me of Rose. I want to tell her I won't be working at the fort anymore, and as we don't own our home here, we will have to move, and that I'm going to find gold to make a better life for her than I gave her mother. Some day she'll understand.

And so I end my contract with the Company and collect my pay. I feel sad leaving the fort men I've worked with for so long. Goodbye to the clerks, and the voyageurs and the carpenters. I'll miss the men I've grown close to — MacKay, my old mentor, and Peopeo, head Hawaiian at the fort. And Como, of course. Most of all, I'll miss Moku.

"The goldfields are no place for a man alone," he says. "Warring Indians, rapids, armed miners. Partner up with someone, for safety."

"If the right man turns up, good and well," I tell him. "If not, I'll go alone. I'd rather have my own poor company than someone I can't get along with." I've thought about it, and there's no one I feel inclined to partner with. I've saved almost enough money for supplies, including a rifle and a good axe, and Neetlum offered his old canoe. It's Salish, and not as large or strong as I'd like, but he doesn't mind when I trade it for a fine Chinook canoe from the Columbia, sturdy and big, with room in it for four men and gear, including extra blankets to trade with the Indians. It's still light enough for me to handle on my own though, and should handle rapids well without tipping. With Neetlum's help, I paint it with ochre and char it, and the canoe looks like new.

I'm working on a plan. I'll need to find work, for it'll take a few more months for me to save the final amount I'll need to buy the last of the supplies for the journey. By then it would be too late in the year to dig, winter being so harsh in the Cariboo, and the ground too cold for working. Yet I don't want to wait till next spring before heading north either, losing precious time and having to fight for claims with the horde of miners arriving after the ground thaws — I need to be there before then, and be ready for when the winter runoff carries the gold down the river. And that means either trekking up in winter, or leaving earlier and wintering over. I don't want to be like those men already coming back, who raced north without forethought or planning. I figure to winter over, build a cabin, make a rocker and sluice box and whatever else I need, and be ready to dig before the surge of miners in the spring crawl over the creeks staking claims.

Kami is asleep, and Moku is with me in my candlelit shack, sitting on an upturned orange box from Spain.

"I never knew you to be foolish, Kimo," he says.

"I won't be gone for long. The California rush soon collapsed. This may not last either. My biggest worry is getting there too late."

"You'll be lucky not to starve, or get scalped."

"I won't be alone. The bars are crowded. And I don't plan to go hungry or lose my hair either."

The next day, when we've finished working the garden, Moku fetches Kami home for me. He's whistling the ballad "Annie Laurie," a tune learned from MacKay. Dusk is creeping over Kanaka Creek so I put Kami to bed and light the candles. Day's end is a time I feel content, when work is finished, and we're fed and warm and dry in the small cabin, with the flickering tapers throwing shadows along the wall.

"I'm coming with you," Moku states with a half grin when I sit down. And I think, surely I've heard wrong. But no. "I'll trek to the Cariboo with you and make enough to come back and buy land here too. Until we return, Khatie will move to the Kwantlen village with Keiki and Kami, and stay with her family. They'll be close to Neetlum and Lawiq'um. Her family will be happy to have her. They spoil Keiki every chance they get. Anyway," he says, "you'll get yourself into trouble without me. You always do."

I laugh. In truth, it's the other way around, for Moku's a magnet for accidents at times. He can cut his wrist just slicing bread. I throw my arms around him and we drink some *tanglelegs* before he sets out for home in the shower of rain that's suddenly falling in great grey splotches, soaking through his wool shirt as he dodges from cedar to cedar.

On the last day to renew contracts, Moku resigns and collects his pay. We sit in the candlelight of my shack, drawing up a list of supplies and costs, and planning strategy for finding gold in the Cariboo. The situation at the Big Canyon is less risky, for things have settled since the Indians gathered to make war against the miners and sent mutilated bodies drifting downriver. The war continues but the body count has dropped. And now the government's new wagon road is well underway. We think we'll paddle as far as Yale, take the wagon road through the canyon, then paddle the river again once we're through. We decide on a leaving date of September, to reach the Cariboo before the worst of winter sets in, and build what we will need to start digging early in spring. And assuming this gift of time hasn't been lent us for nothing, we work for wages in a new sawmill that's begun operating downstream.

And now there's news of a sailor, Billy Barker and six companions, striking more gold this summer at William's Creek. Miners had flocked to the creek earlier when Bill Deitz found gold there, and quickly staked every claim above the canyon. Barker and his partners had no option but to stake below the canyon, putting up with jeers from the men above, but no one's laughing at Billy Barker now. He's pulling out $1,000 a foot of ground. I can't imagine the fortune emerging from that claim. Thousands are flocking to the Cariboo now, and we'll be joining them.

The day we leave there's a wind blowing through Kanaka Creek. The cedar boughs are rising and falling in rhythm, as if something is pulling on them with strings, and all around us are the silt smells of the Fraser, of loamy soil and mist. We make our farewells quickly. We decided that the night before, for it's too painful to drag them out, and weeping will only frighten the children. So we turn and walk away strongly, but Moku is biting his lip so hard the blood starts to dribble down his chin, and my heart is pounding like a drum because Kami is crying after me, and I'm afraid if I don't go quickly, I never will. We reach the loaded canoe and climb in and settle silently among the packs, myself in front, Moku behind. I lift my paddle.

"Ready?"

"Ready," he says, and we move off in tandem, stroking away from the riverbank. Men watch from the other side, from the tents in front of the fort. Somebody waves from the stockade. MacKay shouts, "Watch yer topnotch, now!" and we laugh and wave back at him. But it's a nervous laugh. I remember his advice from years before. "Be prepared for anything. Keep yer mind and knife sharp, and yer powder dry." And decide I'd best not forget any of it.

And so we begin the sixty-mile paddle upriver to Fort Hope. Paddling is easy for us, and cheap. We still plan to abandon the canoe in Yale and make our way on land through the canyon before taking up the paddle again, but we'll be flexible and change plans as circumstances dictate. Adaptability, we've learned, is the key to survival.

After Hope, it'll take a full day to reach Fort Yale and, once past the canyon, it will take eight days paddling to reach the Forks at Lytton, all being well. Which is the best we can hope for, faced with the real probability that things could go far from well in the months to come. Moku reminds me of the dead miner they hauled from the river at Kanaka Creek, and says what we've both been thinking. "If we can hold onto our scalps, we'll do well."

There's a raven flying overhead. Two miles upriver he's still circling. It means nothing, but I wish he'd go away because Moku's superstitious and thinks it's a bad sign.

My crooked finger is sore and stiff from gripping the paddle and the ache makes me think of Rose, who never should have died the way she did. She'd say the bird was telling us something. But what? The pain of losing her still clings, but time has eased the sharpness. I've had no women since Rose died, though there have been village women who showed interest. Or maybe I'm vain to think so. But none I wanted for a wife, or for a mother for Kami. I'm concentrating all my energy into this search for gold. It's going to buy me land and pigs and chickens, maybe even cattle, and a home for my child. I'll be a good father to Kami, a better provider than I was for Rose. And I'll do whatever it takes to get me there. Scalp intact.

chapter five

FOR EVERY CANOE THAT paddles upriver, two come down. The pad-dlers warn that the water's running fast in the canyon. They say every bar is crowded, that it's impossible to stake a new claim. And that the Indians are still killing.

Moku looks at me as if to say, Do we go on or turn back?

"I'm for pushing forward," I say, in spite of the grim news. For if we don't go now, I know we never will. Earlier, we had thought about tak-ing the lake route and coming out at Lillooet, beyond the crowds, for neither of us wanted to face the trials of the canyon. But that would mean back-breaking work of portaging packs and a canoe over the lake trail for more than 100 miles, and we'd rather avoid that.

A mile upriver a clutch of miners hauls a body from the river. We stop, but paddle on because there are men enough to see to it, and soon we reach the mouth of the Harrison River. Here is where miners choosing the lake route leave the Fraser, paddling the narrow stream north into Harrison Lake.

A paddler at the river mouth pulls alongside. His body's covered with ragged clothes. He's filthy. His skin's sallow and his cheeks have sunk. Under a greasy wide-brimmed hat, his hair is pulled back so tight it's drawn his eyes half shut. He looks sick and old, though he might not be. Winter in the Cariboo can add years, they say. He needs a shave and a bath. Our noses know from three feet away.

"The Harrison River's full of shoals," he warns. "The steamer *Queensborough*'s hung up half a mile upstream." We're not surprised. It happens all the time. Their flat bottoms make them bob like ducks in water, and paddlewheels can thrust in only a few inches, but when a sternwheeler gets stuck on a sand bar, it takes a block and tackle to hoist it over the shoals. Steamer troubles are endless. They're always taking holes in their hulls, running short of firewood, even catching fire at times. They can get hung up for hours, or days.

"There's nothing ahead but sandbars, cold and hunger. The Cariboo's a killing place for men. Turn back if you know what's good for you," he says. The man's earnest enough, but our minds are made up. We had decided against taking the lake route anyway, so we bypass the Harrison and paddle on towards Hope.

It's nearly dusk when we arrive. The Hudson's Bay Company built the fort high on a bank near the ancient Sto:lo village of Ts'qu:ls, and we can see the wooden buildings looming dark against the sky ahead of us. The town, another deliberately planted, has blossomed quickly as a stopping point on the supply route to the Cariboo. I like the look of the place, water on two sides, tucked within the mountains at the entry to the canyon at a wide bend in the river.

We follow flickering lights along the riverbank and set up our tent on the shingle, near other men who have pitched tents in rows adjacent to the fort. Fire pits are glowing the length of the beach, like a row of fallen stars, and cooking smells fill the air: beans and bacon and bannock. And fish. Someone's cooking salmon in a pan and it makes our nostrils quiver and saliva glands spurt. I set a fire while Moku throws out a line, and in twenty minutes he's caught a fish.

"Twenty-six inches," he says, stretching it.

"Twenty-two," I counter, and we laugh as I haul out a pan. Nothing tastes as good as fish fried fresh from the water. We eat our fill then walk about the settlement among the men and Indians mingling and drinking and telling tall tales. Beyond the town we can see the Indian village with its cedar longhouse and clustered tepees.

Some of the miners plan to leave at daybreak to head upriver like us, but some are waiting for the steamer *Umatilla* to take them downriver to Langley. It's a filthy thing, tied up at the dock, and crowded with miners sprawling everywhere, some already snoring on floors coated with dirt. It's being mostly wooded up already, for it will burn four cords an hour on its trip downriver.

Din rises from the steamer's decks as men mill about, and from the banter you can tell there's gambling on board. On shore as well, in front of open tent flaps and on makeshift boards under the trees. We join onlookers at the mouth of a tent, where an Indian is squatting on a wool blanket playing cards with a bearded white man wearing a navy pea jacket, and sitting on a flat cedar stump. The Indian is old, and high class, for his forehead slopes back and up to the crown, a status symbol of the local Sto:lo. The white is lean with a windburned face and droopy fair moustache — a middle-aged American by the looks of the Colts fastened at his hips.

"Injun's lost his gun and a heap of pelts," an onlooker says. "He's just bet the woman on the next two throws of the dice. Highest wins." The girl is maybe mid-twenties. She stands behind them, expressionless. She's wrapped in a grey woven blanket, and wears a calf-length deerskin skirt beneath it and leggings and moccasins.

"What's he throwing for?" I ask.

"Tobacco and a sack of tools. Nails, axes, chisels and stuff. He don't even know what all's in the sack."

It's less common now than it used to be for Indians to gamble their house, goods or slaves away, and it draws the crowd. The *haolé* throws first a five, then a four, and calls out "Nine!" through smoke he's puffing from a fine burl pipe, the likes of which I've never seen.

"Do you think tobacco tastes better in a pipe like that?" Moku jabs me with his elbow. Ours are cheap clay. The Indian tosses the dice across the blanket and turns up a four. "The girl just might have a chance," Moku whispers.

The Indian throws again, and the dice turns up three.

"She's mine," the gambler says, cool and calm. He doesn't have to crow over his win, for his right hand rests on his revolver, and the Indian knows there'll be no negotiating over this. He rises from the blanket, turns and walks away without so much as a backward glance at the girl. Her eyes are cast down and she doesn't move, and I wonder at her stoicism. I think about my own part-Indian daughter, and something stabs at me. Moku feels it too, for he steps up to the gambler.

"Let her go," he says, but the man laughs.

"Now why would I do that, friend?" His grey eyes crinkle with amusement.

"She's not store goods or cattle, to be bought or sold or gambled away."

"She's Injun," he retorts, as if that explains everything, and I feel my hackles rise.

"What is she worth?" I step forward. And I know this is not the wisest thing I've done.

"She's not for sale. I'm keeping her," the man says, roughly.

"How much?" I persist.

"How much you got?"

"Enough," I say, though we spent most of our money on gear and have only limited pounds left, and we can't afford to lose any. "I'll toss you for her," I say, regardless.

"Sixty pounds, then?" the gambler says. It's too much to lose, but I can't stop now. Moku is staring at me. The girl lifts her eyes from the ground and stares as well, eyes big as hen's eggs.

"Sixty," I agree. He tosses the dice, and up comes a five, then a four. "Nine," he says. "Your turn."

I roll the dice in my hand, and roll and roll, not wanting to let them go till finally the American loses patience.

"Throw!" he barks, through the tobacco smoke streaming up from his fine pipe, and I roll. And it's a four, and my heart nearly stops. Then the other dice settles and comes up a six and Moku shouts "*Umi!*" Ten. I can't believe my luck.

"She's yours," the gambler says. "A deal's a deal." He rises to leave and the watching miners clap their hands at his show of sportsmanship.

"What if you'd lost?" Moku shakes his head.

"We'd have had a fight on our hands. But we've never lost one yet, have we?"

"The last was ten years ago! Neither of us can move that fast any more."

"Well, it makes no difference. The woman's free." I turn and she's standing next to me. "You can go now," I tell her, raising my arm to wave her away, but she stays where she is, silent, and wide-eyed.

"Speak English?" I ask and she hesitates then nods. "What tribe are you?"

"Tit'a'lit." I've heard this Yale name before. They're Tait Indians. Then she adds "Q'eyts'i," which makes no sense, for Katzie's a down-river tribe, but it doesn't matter because we decide to leave her here and return to our campsite, figuring she'll find her own way home, wherever it is.

We barely reach the camp when daylight suddenly disappears

along the river, as if someone has decided to snuff out a candle, leaving the tiny community in the shadow of the surrounding mountains in a blackness dark as pitch. It brings an end to the hum of activity, to the men's drinking, to their telling of tall tales. The tent city falls silent.

But sleep is broken hours later by rapid shots of gunfire and men's loud garbled shouts. Moku scrambles from the tent to see what the commotion is all about, but I stay put, for I'm tired and cold, and see no point in both of us fumbling about in the dark.

"A black bear," he reports, when he returns. "Roaming the tents. A big one, young, not full grown. Not smart enough to stay with the salmon carcasses on the shingle where they're easy pickings." The bear, it appears, bypassed the fat berry bushes nearby as well, sabotaged by the smell of bacon and fish frying in pans. Moku suddenly stops. "I'm sorry, Kimo. I don't know what I was thinking."

"It's all right. Let's just get some sleep." I don't like bear talk. It was a black bear that killed Rose. She was berry picking with Khatie. The babies were strapped on their backs. They'd been picking an hour or two when Rose screamed, making Khatie stumble and fall to her knees onto the underbrush, spilling her basket and strewing berries across the ground. When something solid hit her square in the chest, her arms instinctively closed round it. It was Kami, crying with fright. Khatie knew why Rose had hurled the baby. She could smell him.

"Run!" Rose flailed her arm towards the river. "Get them away!"

It was a black-brown bear, a female with her tan muzzle up. She stretched her long neck and reared up on her hind legs, growling, giving off a rotten sweet smell. Fear and confusion emanated from the animal. A small cub, no bigger than our own babies, was shuffling at its mother's feet. Bears avoid confrontation more often than not, but a mother with a cub is always dangerous, violent in its protection. The cub's small eyes blinked with curiosity and fear, and it whoofed air noisily from its nose.

"Run!" Rose screeched again. Khatie ran stumbling towards home, clutching Kami to her chest, with Keiki on her back howling in protest. The children bobbled up and down. She had no time to protect them from the rough branches and blackberry thorns blocking their path. When she reached the Kanaka village, the men grabbed rifles and left running. One rowed across the river to the fort to fetch me. By the time we found her, Rose was dead, savaged by the bear, arms and legs torn to pieces. Odd, though, her face wasn't marked. The animal had severed the artery at the back of her neck then left. She died quickly, thank God. I picked her up like a broken doll and carried her home. Her arms and legs, fingers and palms were covered in blood, but there was none on her face. It had all spurted from the gash at the back of her neck. I couldn't bear looking at her. Her lips were drawn back in a peculiar way, almost smiling. I see her that way in my dreams sometimes. But not this night, for I can't sleep. This night, the men have killed the bear, and there is great merriment, and no one can sleep for the rest of the night for talk and *tanglelegs*, and the dead bear grows older and bigger and fiercer with each telling.

Next morning, we wake to the splashes of men bathing along the riverbank — a fine thing, for many of them smell like a dead deer carcass. A good wash is just what they need. We join the swimmers, and everyone complains of the cold, except a few Indians with the group. Indians never feel the cold or damp, it seems. A clutch of miners boasts of lolling in warm water of a natural hot spring in Harrison Lake, but miners, like fishermen, tell tales and no one pays heed. When we return to our campsite, the Indian woman is waiting outside our tent. The old Indian is with her. She draws a woollen blanket tight around her shoulders and steps in front of us.

"*Klahowya*," she says and touches her chest. "Morning Bird."

Then the old Indian steps up. "She belong you, *Oihes. Klosh klootchman. Seokum.* You keep. You win." He says she's a good strong woman and is offended when I say no. His honour is at stake. If I don't keep

53

her, she will have nowhere to go. She is a widow, the wife of his son, and she has no children to care for. He will not have her back. He walks away and the girl remains. I turn to Moku.

"What are we going to do with her?"

"You won her, *aikane*. You think of something."

We figure she'll take off if we just ignore her, so we begin to sort our packs for the next leg of our journey.

"She's hungry," Moku nudges me moments later.

The woman is making feeding motions with her hands. "*Olo?*"

"I suppose we could spare some oatmeal," I say, out of pity for her, for it's a cold day with a keen wind. "Anyhow, we'll need a good feed ourselves for the long paddle ahead."

The woman picks berries while we ready the fire, then takes the pan from me and the wooden stick and the bag of meal and cooks it for us. And the oatmeal is cooked just right, and the tea she makes from the bush berries nearby is sweet and hot. We thank her, but want to be rid of her, for we're heading for the goldfields and the last thing we need is another mouth to feed. I tell her again she must go, but the woman picks up our tin plates and cutlery and walks away. She rubs them in the beach sand and takes them to the water's edge to rinse, and when she comes back she starts to shake out our bedrolls.

"You try." I nudge Moku and he stands full height and points towards the town and tells her forcefully she must stay when we go but the woman named Morning Bird shakes her head.

"I go too," she says simply. But we can hardly hear her because the steamer *Umatilla* chooses that moment to blast its whistle and nearly deafens us. The last cord of wood has been loaded and a trail of tired passengers is struggling up the ramp with their gear. They're miners returning from the Cariboo, weary from the hardships of the river, of the work and the cold, of the mountains and the Indian wars. When the last passenger boards, and the steamer is fully wooded up for New Westminster, the whistle blasts one more time and the sternwheeler pulls away. We turn back to finish speaking with Morning Bird, but she's gone. We're relieved to be rid of her, and set about checking our gear for the journey to Fort Yale. We're tying up our bundles when a pack lands with a thud at our feet.

"Mawnin' Kanakas." The deep voice belongs to Ezekiel Browne. He's been to the goldfields already, he says, to the bars beyond Yale, but cut his hand with an axe. The septic hand wouldn't heal so he couldn't work, and he returned downriver for treatment. Now he's come back, come up on the *Umatilla*, loading cord wood for a cut in the fare. I'm pleased to see the big Negraman.

"I had a partner," he tells us. "A German, named Lickmann. We was headed for the goldfields, but he lost his gear in a poker game, so we split. Now I's stuck here till I find me a new partner. Might take time. Not every man wants to chance it with a Negra."

I catch Moku's eye. He reads my mind and nods. Ezekiel Browne is used to hard labour. He's big and strong and capable. He'd be a good man to have around when trouble comes, as it likely will.

"You can partner with us," I say. "Share the work and pull your weight. No shirking. We get to the Cariboo, we share everything. That's the deal."

The big man cracks a smile and thrusts his black fist forward. "Tha's a deal awright," he says.

"The *wahine*!" shouts Moku suddenly, for there's the woman, Morning Bird, walking along the beach shingle with a bundle tied to her back. "She's back."

"Go away," I tell her, exasperated. "Go home. You're free." I fight not to raise my voice. She doesn't move, so I try again. "It's dangerous. You can't come where we're going." You'd think that would be the end of it, but the woman won't budge. "It's not allowed," I say sternly, as if there were rules set down that must be obeyed, for Indians respect hierarchies and I hope to confuse her.

"Who *tyhee*?" she asks, looking around. She shrugs her shoulders.

But there's no one in sight with any authority. No chief. No one with a tall hat in uniform with braid and brass buttons, no one who looks official. And when the three of us lift our gear into the canoe, she tosses in her bundle and steps in before any of us are off the beach, and reaches for a paddle.

"Out! Now!" I command, but Moku's wearing the look he gets when we don't agree, like he's bit into a bad apple.

"The woman's on her own, Kimo. Abandoned by family and tribe. She could starve. Looks like she can paddle," he adds, for the woman is sitting poised, ready in position. "We could use her help to get to Yale, and let her go there. It's a bustling town and she could find work of some kind, as cook or laundress for someone."

It sounds reasonable to get rid of her in Yale. At least she wouldn't starve. I concede, because it's a long paddle ahead and we must press on. Ezekiel tosses our ninety-pound packs into the canoe and steps in and sits down next to Morning Bird. Moku and I pile in after him. Moku takes the bow paddle, and I have the stern. And as we begin to paddle away from Hope, I think about the twists and turns of life, of how it's a long way from Honolulu to this wild river I'm on, and that there's no turning back now, for I'm on my way to the Cariboo. And the Cariboo gold. With Moku, a black Negraman and an Indian wo-man we can't get rid of. And I wonder what Rose would think of it all.

chapter six

WE PADDLE FASTER THAN the butchers, bakers and candlestick makers calling themselves miners. Ezekiel paddles effortlessly and without complaint. The Indian woman paddles well and doesn't rattle off at the mouth, for which we're all thankful.

Two canoes are ahead of us and more behind, hugging the riverbank. The sky is clear in patches, but there's a breeze, and the dark clouds capping the mountains hint at rain. At noon we aim for the shore. Great boulders rise out of the water, so we paddle till we find a strip of shingle beach where we can pull in safely with the canoe. We chew pemmican instead of cooking, drink from our water flasks and make for the trees. In deference to the woman, we go farther into the trees to relieve ourselves than we would otherwise. By the time we get back, she's sitting back in the canoe, hand on the paddle.

"The wind's changing." Moku tilts his head one way then the other. "We'd better move fast."

The water grows rough. Here and there whitecaps rise, reacting to the wind along the river. The waves swell, and we all feel strain in the shoulders as the canoe loses equilibrium each time a gust hits. The wind funnels between the mountains the length of the river and we have to struggle to hold the craft steady against the current. We paddle close to the bank, but not too close, in case we blow onto the rocks. The woman looks nervous and struggles to maintain her stroke. The canoe heaves up and down on the waves and it's not long before our backs ache and muscles scream, and I'm worried the packs might shift.

Which at least is a sensible worry. I'm not superstitious, though I was when I first came. Back then I would have blamed wind like this on the old Hawaiian gods, or on myself for antagonizing them in some way, though the missionaries taught otherwise. And I'd have prayed to them, making hard-to-keep promises in order to regain their favour. Now I know wind is a force of nature, something natural you deal with, not an unknown directed by the whims of some god turned fickle.

Then, as suddenly as it rose, the wind dies down, and that's the end of it. But we've lost time in the storm and don't stop at the various bars we pass that are being worked. We catch sight of men of every shape and size and age, stooping over pans and rockers, as we paddle on. It'll take all day hard paddling to reach Fort Yale.

Some miles along, we pull over at the biggest bar we've seen. Miners swarm over it like ants. They're American, come up on the trail from Whatcom, all packing revolvers. It's Hill's Bar and they're working it like there's no tomorrow. The air vibrates with expectation. You could grab it with your fist. No one's inclined to talk though, so it's plain we're intruding, interrupting the important business of digging. We move on, leaving them to their pans and pistols.

"I wonder if there's anything left to mine after so many have already worked it?" Moku says.

"Who knows?" I think intelligence might be a part of mining but luck and timing have plenty to do with it. And tenacity pays as well, when gold lies below. We paddle on upriver but it's a battle to move forward against the current now, and our muscles are screaming again. I'm watching now for the rapids I know are ahead. We're nearly there. Paddling downriver, a man can run these rapids safely, but he must know what he's doing. Many have drowned in this white water, their canoes shattered like matchsticks. Moku and I, we've paddled big water in Hawaii, much wilder than this. We've run these rapids before with MacKay, paddling back to Langley after a trek to Yale. Downriver, of course. But we're going upriver now, with a canoe laden with packs.

Morning Bird shouts *"How*! White water!" I listen, and hear a low deep rumble in the distance.

"We had better make for the bank now!" I shout, and we do, fighting our way to shore, where I manage to steer us onto some shingle. We tie up and all four of us sprawl out on the wet stones, hearts pumping, anxious about what's ahead. I don't want us resting and thinking too long though. It'll only make us more edgy. "Let's get through these rapids," I say, speaking with more confidence than I feel. I want them to have no doubts, to stay strong.

"Ready?" They nod.

"Where's our extra rope, Moku? We have to haul now and our bow rope's not long enough."

He retrieves a large coil of rope stowed below the packs. "Got it."

"Tie on a longer length. It has to be long enough to tow all this weight." I sound as if I know what I'm doing. I don't, but McKay at the fort told me how it's done. "Tie another rope midships, Moku. Ezekiel, you have a choice. You can pull behind Moku, or you can get in the canoe with Morning Bird and make sure it doesn't break up along the riverbank while it's being towed. We've got poles to push it off the rocks. We don't want to risk breaking our paddles."

"Ah'd rather haul," Ezekiel says.

"Fine. That'll lighten the load some. I'll pole then, but it might take two of us." I'm anxious, but hiding it. I don't want to scare the woman. "Morning Bird, do you understand?" She nods.

"I come with you," she says quietly, as if this sort of thing happens every day. We clamber back into the canoe. I move the packs to the middle to balance the weight, then pick up one of the six-foot-long poles, and hand the other to Morning Bird. "We have to keep the canoe away from the rocks. Do what I do, as best you can. Understand?"

She nods. I signal Moku.

"Let's go."

He unties the bow rope and the canoe drags for a moment on the shingle then dips and sinks into the river, jigging from side to side as it levels itself. Instantly we drift downriver with the current, alarming Morning Bird.

"Haul away!" I shout, but Moku and Ezekiel are already doing that, putting their backs into pulling the long ropes. Suddenly the ropes take hold and the two of us are thrown forward in the canoe with a jolt. For a second or two it feels as though we're not moving, just pitching up and down on the spot, but then the canoe responds and inches forward, a little at first, but then easier as Moku and Ezekiel manage to find some sort of rhythm.

Moku's a few feet in front of Ezekiel. They're walking ahead of us, on the riverbank, leaning their bodies forward, straining hard as horses. Slowly and steadily we head for the rapids. When we reach the white water, I pole frantically against the rocks littering the riverbank to keep the canoe from crashing into them, and so does Morning Bird. We heave up and down, pitching and rising, again and again. The canoe's filling with water. It's ice cold, slapping around our ankles.

We keep poling hard while Moku and Ezekiel haul, bent double with the effort. They've wound the ropes around their waists, twisted them around their right wrists to prevent slipping, and are tugging the ropes over their right shoulders. Thank God for their strength. Heads down, muscles straining, they're hauling us along like those old Clydesdales do at the fort.

"Pole!" I yell at Morning Bird, whenever we near the rocks, and we push and shove hard to keep the canoe safe. Moku and Ezekiel strain forward still. Suddenly we're through and it's over. We're in calmer water. The men haul a few hundred yards more before Moku waves and hauls us ashore where it's clear of rocks. We tie up. We feel good.

"It wasn't as hard as I figured," I say.

"You weren't the horse!" Moku retorts. We laugh. Nerves, I suppose. Relief, at any rate.

Morning Bird helps me bail out the inches of cold water dumped in the canoe. The packs are soaked, and so are we. Buckskin gets hard and scratchy when it gets wet, so she'll be uncomfortable real soon.

"Good, no rain," she says, with an eye to the clear sky overhead, looking on the bright side, I suppose. I think that's all we'd need: to be hauling a canoe through rapids in a thunderstorm. After bailing as much as we can from the canoe, we reload the packs and take up our paddles again. An hour later, we reach Fort Yale as dusk is creeping across the sky. It's a small post, established on orders from Mr. Douglas in 1847 but now it's mobbed with near twenty thousand miners. After hauling the canoe up on the shingle, Moku and I leave Ezekiel and Morning Bird to set up camp while we head out to find our friend, Ovid Allard, who is in charge of this fort.

Ovid arrived in Langley just after I did but left later after a dispute with Mr. Yale over something I don't remember . . . dogs come to mind. But now the big man's come back to run the town and deal with the influx of miners. And Indians, for he speaks several of their dialects.

We find him in his quarters, where his wife serves us a tasty venison stew. She's a small, dark-eyed native woman, quick smiling, wearing a European-style dark blue cotton dress. Her actions are unhurried but precise and she moves with a grace that reminds me of the women of Hawaii. It occurs to me while I'm filling my stomach that Ezekiel and Morning Bird are making do with less at the camp, but hunger and the Allards' welcome suppress my niggles of guilt.

"The Americans would turn the town into their own Wild West if we let them," Ovid says, "shooting guns at the drop of a hat, swaggering 'round town like they own the place." The big man is stressed. I notice his bushy eyebrows have grown back since they were singed off years ago during the old fort fire, when he ran into a burning shack to rescue the dairyman's baby.

"The Fraser's bars are full. The Thompson's filling fast. Men are crawling along Quesnelle creeks like ants. A town is growing around Billy Barker's find. If you're going to Barkerville, there's a stage running north now. It's safer than trekking up on your own. The wagon road's a hellhole in places, with men and mules falling off Jackass like flies."

For that's the story of the mining camps, that Jackass Mountain has the steepest grade on the wagon road. That so many mules have fallen off it, they named the mountain after them. The road is scraped out of steep precipices that drop sharply to the river. There are no barriers to protect you. No one dares travel it after dark. And neither man nor beast has survived falling off it into the river.

"It'll be too expensive," Moku says. "Besides, I'd rather take my chance on foot than sit in a stage somebody else is driving on a narrow cliff edge."

"Well, one way or another, you need to get over Jackass," Allard says. "After the canyon, you can paddle again, but it's not easy. Only one in four are making it upriver."

With Ovid's words ringing in our ears, we feel unsettled on our trek back to camp. We think riding the stage all the way is out of the question. It would eat too much into our budget.

"There's no use spending good money if we don't have to. As soon as we get over Jackass, we can take to the river again. Wasn't that the plan?"

It was. So we stick with it. And how many of life's decisions are made this way, I wonder, paths chosen, destinies altered, because of money, or more often, the lack of it?

We don't talk of the men who didn't make it, the starved, bloated bodies floating down the river, or the remains of miners, scalped and mutilated, drifting downstream lodging among the reeds along the river's banks. But I think about them, and know Moku does too, in spite of the merry jig he starts whistling.

Ezekiel and Morning Bird are huddled by the fire when we return. Ezekiel has wrung the heads off two squirrels, stuck them on a stick and roasted them over the fire, to save our packed grub, so I worried for nothing, for they've eaten their fill. And now we sit and exchange stories. There's nothing like a campfire to make people weave their pasts into tales, true and otherwise.

Moku rises in the Hawaiian way, and speaks of his birth in Kailua. He talks of Khatie, his Kwantlen wife, of his daughters, now married, of his young son, Keiki, and of his life at Kanaka Creek, across from the Langley fort.

I say I too was born in Hawaii, that my life is like Moku's, but my wife is dead, and I have a daughter named Kami.

"I was born Q'eyts'i," Morning Bird says when Moku presses her. Like many Sto:lo, the people of the river, she speaks her own Halq'emeylem, along with Chinook, a mix of native, English and French words. Many natives living near forts speak English now. Keen traders, they learned quickly. She's taller than most Indian women, about five foot eight, and carries herself well. Her black hair is tied in two bunches with thin strips of hide strung with blue beads. She has high cheekbones and dark Indian eyes, turned down in folds at the outside. They're large and intelligent looking. Her nose is fine, slightly hooked, not flat like some. She's a fine looking woman. She's changed into dry clothes. Her buckskin is drying on a stick rack beside the fire.

"You're a long way from home. How did you get here?" She takes so long to answer, I think she hasn't heard me.

"I was captured in a Lekwiltok raid and traded to a man of the Tit'a'lit wanting a wife. I was thirteen." She falls quiet then adds, "for two blankets and a rifle. He treated me well enough, though he had other wives, one before me and a young one after. I had a child, a girl. She died of the pox last winter, along with her father." Just like that she says it, and turns away so we can't see her expression, then falls into silence like a fire dying down. What can you do when you're taken by force and made to live a life not of your choosing, bearing a child and losing her, and being unwanted in a tribe where you're to be used or spent like a coin? She turns away and I don't know what to say to her. None of us do.

Ezekiel coughs and our attention is drawn back to the fire, away from the woman, and it's a kindness he's done.

"How old are you, Ezekiel?" Moku asks. It's hard to tell. He could be twenty-five or fifty.

"Forty somethin', ah think. I was born in the springtime. My mammy was weedin' the fields at the time and took the colic and ett some calamus root for pain and after that, I was born. Weedin' the ground is done afore plantin' so that's how I know it was springtime."

But I'm thinking, a freed slave should have papers signed by the owner who freed him, with particulars about his origins and name and age. Moku asks him about mining, for we two know only what we've picked up from the men passing through. He details for us different colours of sand and bedrock and pay stratum and rockers and sluices. He confirms what we've heard about rules for registering; a claim must be twenty-five feet wide at high water, marked with two pegs at least twelve inches high, squared off to four inches at the top. It has to be pegged again two more times along the direction of the claim lines. Bar diggings should measure twenty-five feet at the top, with the strip of land extending to the river's low-water mark. We had an idea of the process, but it's a comfort having Ezekiel with us, for he knows particularities we don't, having been to the bars already. We do know that we need to get a number from the nearest gold commissioner to write on our claim pegs, when and where we want to stake a claim. And we know all the lower bars are spoken for.

"How far north we going then?" Ezekiel asks. "Barkerville? William's Creek?"

"Don't know for sure," I say. "There's plenty creeks up there never seen a spade yet."

The Negraman is not intrusive or loud, and there's a great strength in him that has nothing to do with physical size. He's done carpentry, which will be handy when we need to build equipment and shelter. He's mined and farmed in his time. He's worked the docks in San Francisco. I recall he even mended his boots at the fort — I think there's not much this big Negraman can't turn his hand to.

"Must've been hard, being a slave," I say, but it's a witless thing I've said and I regret it the minute it spills from my mouth. Ezekiel's white teeth flash in a grimace.

"A man don't fo'get some things," he says, massive chest heaving. His dark eyes bulge like hens' eggs, the surrounds whiter than white as he stares into the fire. He doesn't blink an eye, just stares as if in a trance. His hair is black as ink, and it curls in tiny corkscrews all over his head. His head is square and sits on wide shoulders, on a neck thick as a tree trunk. His nose is wide and flat, as if it's been broken, and I suspect he's seen some fighting in his time. His hands are broad and calloused, fingers thick as bananas, and the backs of his hands are stubbled with hair like a newly plucked chicken. His thick lips tighten for a fraction of a second, and I don't know what's behind the mask, for that's what he seems to wear now as we sit by the fire, flames darting here and there making angles and shadows over his cheekbones.

"My pappy was a Lomboko man," he says, and repeats it sing-song, as if reciting a poem. "He told me never to forget the name. That he was a man from Lomboko. Across the ocean somewheres."

I never heard the name before but guess it's on the West African coast, where the slave traders go. They chain black men, women and children, herd them onto stinking ships and sell them like cattle — those who survive the hellish journey — to be slaves in the Carolinas. Ezekiel's voice changes. It sounds like it's coming through a tunnel.

"They tied my pappy to a tree and kilt him. For no reason, jus' nigger huntin'. He was offa the property, on a errand. They got him in the face with some shot and left him to die tied to that old tree. But he lived for days, my pappy, he was that strong, so they come back and beat him till he done up and died. How kin a man disremember sech a thing? Or his mammy sold off, gittin' branded on her breast and atween her shoulders, so sore it just about kilt her?"

I stand fixed as a post, feeling about for words, but there's none I can find that would make the Negraman feel less pain. I'm truly sad about his father, and wish there was some way of giving comfort, but no man has the key to another's distress. I look at the Indian woman and think she can stay, if that's what she wants, for I've no stomach for making anyone's life worse than it is.

When I tell Moku, he's not so sure it's a good thing, but figures she'll be useful around the camp for her keep. But we don't want her sleeping in our tent, so Ezekiel moves his gear into ours to allow the woman to occupy his. She's up before we rise in the morning, with a fire going and oatmeal stirring in a pan. She's determined to cook and clean for us. I suppose it's bred into a slave to do for folks. Ezekiel treats her kindly.

When I tell Morning Bird she can stay, she looks at me as if I'm crazy. Clearly she had no intention of doing otherwise. I feel a surge of irritation. Why won't the woman return to the Q'eyts'i where she was born, or even go back to the Tait? She's free yet moves about her chores as if she's still a slave. Years of bondage maybe does it. Freezes feeling till you have no wants of your own. I knew a dog like that once, tethered all its life. When they cut its rope, it wouldn't budge, just ran in the same circle it was used to running. I wonder if Morning Bird will be like that old dog, or if she'll manage to break her invisible chains — and if so, how long it will take her.

chapter seven

ROSE COMES TO ME in the night. I can hardly breathe, I'm so full of joy at seeing her. It's been so long since her last visit and she comes to me softly, wearing her long blue cotton dress, the one with the white collar she sewed herself with fine needles and thread from the fort. The white of the collar contrasts with the deep bronze of her skin and her long black hair. The tiny wooden dolphin, the good luck charm carved by my Hawaiian *kupuna*, is tied around her neck on its narrow leather thong, and pink shells dangle from her ears. Her eyes are dark and luminous as she lies down beside me and I long to sink into her. She's sad that I've left Kami. "I'll go back for her," I promise. Too soon, she's rising to leave and my heart aches and cries out *Don't go, don't go*, but her feet, her body, her face, her eyes melt away slowly, and Moku and Ezekiel, who were gone in the dream, are suddenly back in their blankets, snoring loudly.

I lie awake, imagining she's still with me. I reach to touch her, my eyes look for her, my ears want to hear her breathing beside me. I miss the scent and touch of her skin. But she's gone, and won't come back. After a time I fall into sleep, down the steep well of dreams into darkness deep as the sea.

In the morning we check our supplies, food, shovels and pans. We plan to set out on the wagon road at dawn but Ezekiel suggests we first buy another sheet of tin with perforated holes for the rocker, in case the one we have gets ruined. We head into town. The tin sets us back two dollars.

Moku decides to pick up some ship's biscuits. "We'll need them if we hit a bad patch," he says. Myself, I never want to set my teeth into one again. On the ship from Honolulu, they were so full of weevils, the crew laid bets on which of them would scurry across the table fastest. But he's happy with his purchase and tucks the tin inside his pack.

Yale is full of something. Promise, hope . . . it hovers in the air and it's palpable. It touches you, makes your skin tingle. Indians and whites mingle on the streets — if you can call them streets —Americans add their own zest to the mix of humanity, and the air's explosive. Here's another *haolé* town sprung up and spread over the landscape quick as a weed. Parallel to the river, on Front Street, there's the small Hudson's Bay fort: no stockade, just a single log building, now also a store. There's a post office and shops, and bars and eating places crowded with miners, a weaving of noises and smells. The bars are busy, in spite of drunks on the street complaining of watered-down beer. There are a few women, good and otherwise, walking the boards in hoopskirts.

A few shops farther down there's Barnard's Express Office, more stores, and saloons one after the other, as far as the eye can see. Four parallel streets cut at right angles by four parallel streets — that's Yale. Between and behind the clutter of storefronts perches a colony of miners' tents and crudely made whipsawn shacks, set every which way but straight up with hardly a square angle in sight. The gold commissioner's office is crammed already with miners lined up half a block long outside.

They're an odd mix of humanity. One man wears a sergeant's uniform. A miner tells us it's from the Crimean war. Another's wearing galoshes, leaning aristocratically on a cane, sporting a dandy weskit over a frilled muslin shirt, with a sword buckled at his waist. Maybe he's planning to duel his way through the Cariboo. There are men with wool pants tucked into their socks just below the knee, wearing red and black checkered shirts from the fort's store. Whiskered faces hide beneath wide-brimmed slouch hats, and they wear revolvers on their hips the way women wear jewellery. They use them to shoot each other or to punctuate conversation when the mood — or the drink — takes them.

Anxious to get underway, we return to camp. Ezekiel and Morning Bird are sitting on the last of the packs. The beach is deserted, the nearby miners having left at dawn. I'm cramming the last of our gear into the packs, when *ping* — a sharp crack rings out. Crows explode from the treetops, cawing and chirping with fright, and Morning Bird yelps then stumbles, clutching at her shoulder.

"She's hit!" Moku rasps. We drop to the ground, scanning the beach and the far side of the river for signs of a gunman. The woman's on her knees now, Ezekiel beside her. Blood is seeping through her deerskin dress.

I crawl over to the woman. She's biting her lip and trembling like a birch in the wind. Her shoulder's seeping blood, the thin red stream darkening as it spreads.

"Where is he?" Moku crawls along the ground with his rifle.

"Can't tell." There's no sign of any marksman. There's no second shot. We fan out slowly, but find nothing. No sound of movement from the undergrowth, no leaves shifting, no branches breaking, no glint of a rifle barrel. Just silence. I crawl back to the woman. She's breathing heavily. There's a hole where the bullet tore through the deerskin and I tear at it, ripping it wide to expose the wound. There's an inch-long burn mark along the bone, red and black and purple, from the bullet grazing her clavicle, but it didn't penetrate the bone. The woman sits up, breathing unsteadily, but I'm surprised by her composure. No wailing, no tears, though her lashes look dark, as if they could spill over any minute.

"Anyone got reason to shoot at you, Morning Bird?"

"No," she shakes her head.

"Anything in that bag of yours that might not belong to you?"

"No. Just food, enough for a few days."

Moku gives me the eye. He's sorry the woman is hurt, as we all are, but he's thinking what I'm thinking. How can she work or be useful now, with a wound in her shoulder? She curls inside the grey wool blanket that Ezekiel pulls from his pack. We listen for her breathing to even out.

"We should take her back to the fort," I say. "She needs fixing. Who could have done this?"

Moku squats beside me. The woman's gone quiet. Her head's drooping and she's shaking. Shock is setting in.

"Somebody's as like shot his gun for no good reason," Ezekiel says. "Jes drunk, shootin' for the sake of it. You seen 'em. They'll shoot at anything: birds, skunks, squirrels, movin' shadows."

"Maybe," Moku says, "or it could be the Indians. Some of the tribes are still angry. With all these miners pushing through the mountains, I'd be surprised if they're not drawing a line again to stop folk moving deeper into their territory."

Unless it was a mistake, for Indians are laying down their bows and arrows for rifles and, like the miners, they don't all know how to use them. Rifles go off half-cocked more than enough.

"Aw, shit!" Moku says. "We'll be sitting ducks out on the river if there's still Indians out there wanting to kill miners." We sit quiet a while.

Ezekiel finally says, "We need to git to the Cariboo. That don't change."

"But we have to get there all in one piece," Moku insists. "What use is it if one of us gets shot up and can't work a shovel?" We sit for a while in silence till Moku rises to his feet. "Ovid was right. Can we afford to take the wagon road?"

"We can't afford the stage coach, if that's what you mean."

"I mean trekking up on foot. We'll be safer in the middle of a pack of mules and miners than in a canoe on the river. We were paying to freight our gear over Jackass anyway. Can we afford to freight farther?"

"It depends on what they're charging."

"We kin find out." Ezekiel says. He agrees with Moku.

"Later. Right now we need to get this *wahini* some help." I hunker beside Morning Bird. Her eyelashes look heavy and wet with tears but her cheeks are dry. She just won't let the tears go. Her wound isn't serious, thank goodness. The bullet didn't enter, just grazed her clavicle, but she's bleeding from the skin tear — more than I would've figured, though I'm no expert on gun wounds. I probe the clavicle and she flinches. It's not broken, but I think I see the trace of a crack. Not much, but enough to hurt like hell.

"You's one lucky woman," Zeke says. "A snick either way, you'd be in real trouble."

"Can you stand, Morning Bird?" She nods. "Good. Hold on." Moku helps me lift her to her feet. "We'll get you back to the fort. You'll be all right. It'll heal quickly." I truly feel badly for her, but honestly I'm relieved she'll have to stay in Yale.

Ezekiel stays with our packs while Moku and I take Morning Bird to the fort. We find the Allards. Mrs. Allard cleans Morning Bird's

73

wound. Ovid sprinkles a grainy white powder on it from a wooden chest stored beneath his bed and ties a triangle of clean white cloth around her neck to lay her arm in to relieve pressure on the clavicle. His wife brews willow bark tea for Morning Bird, who sips it quietly and soon the shaking eases.

"You didn't see the shooter at all, Kimo?"

"Saw nobody. Heard nothing after the shot. Only one was fired."

"Likely some upriver Indian with a grudge, ignoring the peace treaty."

We tell Morning Bird to stay in town to recuperate. She thanks Mrs. Allard for her help and walks out the door. Moku looks like he's ready to say something but doesn't. I feel rattled and guilty for setting the woman loose in her condition but relieved at the same time, since we're back on track for the Cariboo.

We return to the river bank only to find the woman sitting with Ezekiel by our packs. I tell her again to go home, that we are selling the canoe to raise money to buy freight tickets for the Wagon Road. She leaves, and we start shifting the packs to tote them over to the Express ticket office. But before we're done, she's back, with two stocky Indians in tow.

"Crow Man and Yellow Hawk," she says. "They come back from Cayoosh. They pay good, buy our *kanim*."

"MY canoe," I remind her. The two Indians are Kwantlen, in Yale after leading a party of miners upcountry to Lillooet. It's a fact, the tribes are as enterprising as the Company when opportunities present themselves. Along the river, people depend on friendly natives for paddling miners and their gear to and fro, and leading parties through the mountains. Natives are even piloting the river steamers. I know we could find buyers for our canoe in town, but it'll take time. So I dicker, expecting them to trade, but they surprise me and flash American dollars, so we make a deal. They'll sell the canoe before the day is out for more than they've paid me, I'm sure.

"Morning Bird, you understand you can't come with us? The long trek would be too hard on you." I don't want her to leave empty-handed, or going hungry either, so I forage in my pack and pull out two packs of dried food for her, pemmican and cranberries. "Here, take these." I hand her some dollars too. "Thanks for your help selling the canoe. I hope you get well soon, and find work here." She accepts the dollars and food packs and nods her thanks, then turns and walks away with Crow Man and Yellow Hawk.

We head for the freight train office. Since the opening of the wagon road, the price of packing has dropped from ninety to fifty cents a pound, good news for us. There's a poster on the wall for the new stagecoach being brought into service soon. They say that it's red with yellow running gear and it'll take only four days to reach Soda Creek. It's a fine coach, to be hauled by a team of four horses, carrying fourteen passengers. Fare $130 apiece. You'd need big money to afford the ride. It'll be much faster than the two-horse stage that runs now, though.

We're paying for packing only. That lets us walk with the freight wagons, three ten-tonne wagons pulled by oxen, and four dozen pack mules carrying from 250 to 400 pounds apiece. Everyone's heading to the new towns of Clinton, Quesnelle and Barkerville, the desk clerk tells us, since Billy Barker hit pay dirt by William's Creek. He says five thousand people have rushed up that creek already. So we're going as far as money will take us from the crowded bars of the Fraser, to the northern Cariboo creeks. We can afford to freight as far as 150 Mile House, and we can trek to Barkerville from there. The mile houses are measured from Lillooet, where the Harrison Lake route to the Cariboo joins the Wagon Road.

We bind up and weigh our packs, what we're not carrying. We've packed flour, dried fruits such as apples and cranberries, oatmeal, candles, soap, lard, condensed milk, onions, tea and coffee, matches, bacon and beans. Lots of beans. And extra clothing, boots, shovels, pans, axes and saws for making sluice boxes. I ask the wagon master if they need any carpenters, as wheels might need fixing on the way and we could use the money, but no. They have all they need. We sleep on the beach, waiting for the wagon train to leave next morning.

Rose comes in the night, whispering on the wings of sleep. I no longer rebuke myself for her death, for not achieving the long happy marriage we planned. She's glad my spirit has returned, dispersing the cloud of unreason that had numbed my soul. I vow to secure my survival for Kami's sake and not leave her fatherless. I've walked that road, and won't have it for my child. Rose is pleased and I drift into sleep and find myself home in the South Seas, in a world of sweet scented frangipani and blue skies, of palms rustling in the trade wind breeze, of warm sand and the shush of the ocean sweeping Oahu's shore, and Kami's gurgling laughter echoing in my brain.

By five a.m., Front Street is jostling with people claiming seats on wagons, toting bulging carpet bags and afterthought bundles, pasts securely contained and tied with string, to be let loose sometime, someplace.

"Wagons ho!" The bullslinger's voice echoes the length of the street. He stands, feet apart, in the middle of the road, cracking a whip. I expected a big man, powerful and strong, but he's small and wiry and his narrow shoulders don't fit inside his unbuttoned long coat. He's wearing a narrow-brimmed stiff hat and high-topped, flat-heeled calf-skin boots tucked into his pant legs. He's packing a rifle, and I'm glad he's armed. A gun in the right hand is worth a few inches of stature any day. He smacks the air and the whip's leather strap snaps down the row of oxen, stopping inches away from the bulls' noses. They heave their big backs on cue and begin to lurch up Front Street, north onto the Cariboo Wagon Road.

We head for Spuzzum and the new Alexandra Suspension Bridge, and after forty-four miles we'll reach Jackass. It'll be a challenge crossing that mountain, so many men and mules having toppled off the damn thing. But I have a good feeling about things. Here I am, trudging alongside a ten-tonne wagon, on our way to the Cariboo, with Zeke and Moku, who's whistling off key that comic tune they're singing in the taverns, "Old Rosin the Beau."

When I'm dead and laid out on the counter,
A voice you will hear from below,
Saying, send down a hogshead of whiskey,
To drink with old Rosin the Beau,
To drink with old Rosin the Beau,
To drink with old Rosin the Beau,
Saying, send down a hogshead of whiskey,
To drink with old Rosin the Beau.

But I'm wondering what happened to the Indian woman. I should've been kinder to her. That bullet she took, was it a random shot or was it meant for her? She claimed to have no enemies. As far as I know, Moku and Zeke don't have any either. That leaves me with Ahuhu. He is a sick man, with a twisted mind who'd like nothing better than put a bullet in me. But imagination can play tricks on you. Likely it was just some drunk letting off steam. People get killed here for the least vexation. Reason has no place in Yale, a town gone mad for gold. Civilized conduct's been cast off like unwanted clothing, and innocents like Morning Bird suffer for it. We haven't seen her since we sold the canoe. I hope she'll find her family and return home safely. That's my hope for all of us, as we head to the Cariboo.

chapter eight

THE BARNARD'S EXPRESS stage has left ahead of us with its three passengers and the driver. Behind the freight wagons and walking miners, other families prepare to leave in their own wagons. "Prairie schooners," they call them, farm wagons with a flat bed, made of hardwood and covered with canvas. They're only about ten feet long by four feet wide, but they're loaded with cargo. Two of the newer wagons have passenger seats. Some wagons are crammed with miners, others with Chinamen. There are family wagons with women and children inside. There's one being driven by a seaman, with two frock-coated gentlemen inside, and another with men in soldier's uniforms.

In another, an American is travelling with four women. Soiled doves, we suspect, but Zeke says they're hurdy gurdy girls from California, following the miners here now that the '48 gold rush has run out.

"German dancin' women," Zeke explains. "Hurdies. Wild, feet up in the air dancin', to barrel organ music. I seen a real hurdy gurdy once. It's a wheel fiddle you crank, that makes a dronin' sound. The hurdies charge a dollar a dance and you have to buy drinks for yourself and them too. They ain't all soiled doves," he says, "but in the right saloon, you can pay extra for private favours, if you's so inclined."

We're not, but we look the women over. They're older than we first suppose. Two are German, two Dutch. They look buxom and sullen and overfed on potatoes. Any man dancing them around would need strong biceps. I don't know what would bring them on the wagon road, for there's no saloons yet where we're going, just roadhouses for travellers to eat and sleep. But it'll come to that soon enough. The American has figured that out, I suppose. But I wonder what pulled these women to California in the first place, to place their lives in the hands of such a man.

The wagon behind us is driven by a middle-aged Englishman named Thomas Hawthorn. He's tall and thin, with dime-size blue eyes and a tuft of blond hair wisping down his forehead. His wife and four-year-old son are with him, and his pale younger brother, Nelson, drives a second wagon loaded with household goods and a small piano. As if a cabin in the Cariboo can be furnished like an English manor. But at the Langley fort, there was once a wife who didn't scrub floors or cook but painted pretty flowers and stitched fine pictures with a needle. She was a sweet thing, skin transparent white as the thin porcelain cups she drank from, and she sang like a bird. This was what she knew, what made sense of her world. So I suppose a piano might make sense in the Hawthorns' world, giving them comfort when the wilderness closes in, as it surely will. Myself, I'd swap it for a rifle.

I scan the other walkers but see no familiar faces among the miners, teamsters and swampers. It's a hard twelve miles to Spuzzum. The trail's a good eighteen feet wide, enough for a wagon train to turn around. The Royal Engineers blasted it from the canyon walls only months ago, and built and levelled it across the steep gullies. So here we are walking upon this wagon road as if it had always been, and it leads us straight to the new Alexandra Suspension Bridge across the river between Spuzzum and Chapman's Bar.

I've never seen such a bridge before. I've seen ropes thrown over streams, and logs laid across them, but it takes your breath away that men can create such a structure. They say it spans 269 feet. It's made of iron, with great cables of wire, and it looks both frail and strong at the same time, a thin ribbon arcing across the swirling waters below. It's beautiful. And terrifying. I want to remember it, every grey line, every stretched silver wire, with the river snaking and snarling below, and great trees rising like warrior spears along the mountainsides. The current rages, hurtling through the canyon with a noise like thunder.

We get soaked from the heavy drizzle that's been falling like rods for the last hour, and our feet slide on the iron decking, but we cross safely, the animals, the wagons, the walkers. I tell myself the great bridge must be safe, but I feel an aching relief when we leave it behind. We've covered fifteen miles, and night is falling when the train stops at one of the new roadhouses.

We're weary from the day's walk, and wet. The horses are neighing and the mules braying as the swampers rush to tie them up. Travellers make for the roadhouse. It's full so some of us have to camp outside, which at least saves us the dollar each it costs for a bed and meal. It's raining, but the place springs to life as people drift about with water buckets and bundles, acquainting themselves one with another, hunching shoulders against the wind and wet drizzle. Smoke and bacon smells rise from the roadhouse chimney and drift our way, making our mouths water. A figure steps up to our campfire. I can't believe my eyes when I recognize Morning Bird through the smoke. She's wearing a European style calf-length grey calico dress and she has three small children in tow.

"What are you doing here?"

"I find work in Yale," she says proudly. "I come with the Hesse family. German, up from Oregon. *Kloochman* is sick. I cook and clean for them, look after children."

The German is planning to farm north of Clinton, she tells me, and she will stay there with the sick woman and children, two girls and a boy, while he returns to Oregon for Texas longhorn cattle, which he will drive up later in the spring. Suddenly the German calls her and she leaves with her water bucket, the children trailing behind. We watch the family climb the roadhouse stairs. Morning Bird, too. I'm glad they didn't leave her to sleep in the wagon. That shoulder must still hurt, though she's not wearing Allard's sling any more — a good sign.

Our fire mutinies and won't stay lit in the drizzle. Impatient and hungry, we eat beans before they're cooked through. Raindrops sizzle in the pan along with the fat and keep the bacon from crisping so we settle for soggy bacon, dried fruit and Moku's hard biscuits, which taste better than I remember. There's a keen wind, and cold invades the tent, chilling us through. Moku and I had plenty of practice sleeping out as Bay men. Knees raftered up in the cold, listening to the rainwater trickling down the tent canvas, we fall asleep. Zeke, though, doesn't shut an eye. His southern soul isn't used to the cold yet.

In the morning we rustle up some oatmeal. The smell of hot coffee and bacon and eggs cooking tantalizes us, creeping our way every time someone opens the roadhouse door. Snow mixed with rain dampens our fire, and we fight to keep it lit.

"Sickness will hit us if this weather keeps up," Moku says. "It'll get worse the farther north we go. We should make sure we get into the roadhouses from here on. We want to eat and sleep indoors when it's wet and cold like this, and to hell with the cost. We can't afford to get sick."

"Thas right," Zeke says. "Digging gold is back-breaking. We need to stay strong." He hasn't stopped shivering. We have the canoe money, and the packing costs were less than we figured, so I don't argue the point. They're right. Staying well is a priority. So it's settled. We'll make sure we find beds inside at the next stopovers.

Morning Bird appears, skirting the miners, heading for our campfire. She draws something from her pocket and hands it to me then walks away. I open the small brown paper package to find three large hotcakes bigger than my fist. They're warm, golden brown, light and airy, and we cram them into our mouths and chomp them down. I don't know if she stole the food for us this morning from the roadhouse or if it was left over at the breakfast table. No matter, it's a kindness.

We head out for Hell's Gate, feeling sleepless and tired after our cold night. Again I'm taken aback by what the *haolés* have done to this place. The wagon road has been ripped from the side of the steep mountain, suspended with earth and cribbing over the raging river below. Zeke's eyes are big as coconuts.

"Sneeze and we'll be over the edge in the blink of an eye," he says.

We're not the only ones feeling nervous. Miners are eyeing each other, mumbling oaths and prayers. I say one myself. The oxen slow to a snail's pace and the horses up front step gingerly as their driver reins them in tight. The mule skinners loosen their lines and set the mules in pairs, to let them find their own sure-footed way along the trail. Those of us on foot have space to shift close to the mountainside, away from the sheer drop. It's all uphill and treacherous underfoot, but on we go, on and up. I break out in a sweat. We have to carry what we need on the trek, for there's no access to the gear you pay to freight. So my back's sore, my heart's pounding, and I can feel the throb in my ears. Moku is having to take deep breaths to steady himself. Zeke's skin is shining with sweat. The river is racing below us, roaring like thunder, pounding against the canyon walls.

Looking down makes you dizzy so I look straight ahead. Miners in front of us keep stumbling. Those not able to cope with the climb drop back. We pass them and plod on, placing one foot before the other in the dirt of the trail, concentrating on the stones beneath our feet so that we don't slip. Breath leaves my cracked lips, misting out before me like smoke in the cool air, sending silent messages of thanks upwards to the gods. To the old Hawaiian gods, and the Christian God, for helping us decide on the road route. The river is hellish here. Its crushing power could shatter a canoe to matchsticks. How many souls have been swallowed up by this canyon, I wonder? Fathers lost, husbands drowned, families torn asunder?

The wagon train's gone silent. The noise of water thundering against the canyon walls awes everybody. The drivers look drawn, lips pursed, concentrating on navigating the wagons as close to the mountainside as possible. The immense trees cast black shadows forward as the mules and oxen pass, and the heavy scent of wet cedar and pine permeates the air we breathe. But then at long last we're through, and after a brief rest, the train moves on towards China Bluff.

Chinamen are digging for gold here. They are strange and secretive, these yellow people, crawling like busy ants on the banks below. White miners have panned here already and moved on, but the Chinamen are searching for what's left along the riverbank. Some have come up from California. Others came as cheap labour first there and now here. Life's hard for them. I hope the yellow men find some gold. Every colour of man deserves a chance to fulfill his dream.

The train moves on towards Boston Bar, which is full of Americans with their tents pitched right next to the old Indian village. We pass through, and the wagons halt at the next roadhouse. Above a plank door, deer antlers hang from a pine slab. The miners who slept in the wind and rain last night clamour for a dry bed inside. The place is crowded to the rafters and the beds are quickly taken. Those without have to sleep on and under tables made of twelve-feet-long planks, and on the floor. The place is clean enough, but reeks of sweat and leather and the nose-tingling smell of wood smoke from the fire. And whiskey fumes, for some of the men have warmed their insides already, and are fighting over bed space.

It costs us $1 for the night, including food. The meal is surprisingly good, with pork and beefsteak for dinner, potatoes and vegetables, puddings, hot rolls and butter and cream, all laid out in big platters to help yourself. We sit on worn wooden benches, eating our fill and feeling like kings.

The hurdy gurdy girls sit across from Morning Bird and the Hesse family. The father looks solemn and preoccupied. His wide-eyed children are wary, eyeing the curious assortment of humanity lurching around them. Their pale mother is on edge, distracted by the road-house din. She's a delicate woman, and the unexpected screech of a chair leg scratching the floor makes her jump a foot. They've all got beds. We don't, but we sleep well on the floor anyway, exhausted from the day's climb, warm dry air wrapping round us like a blanket.

I drift off and meet Kami in my dreams, perched on a grey boulder on the river shingle. She's looking upriver, watching, waiting for something or someone, twisting nettle stems into twine, the way her mother taught her. Small dark birds pick between the stones at her feet, white heads bobbing, unafraid. She rises suddenly and heads into the woods, and I wake with fright, calling her name. I toss and turn the rest of the night, sleepless, till the proprietor rings the bell for breakfast. The smell of coffee permeates the roadhouse as a feast of hot porridge, bacon and beans, pies and pancakes is laid out. Din escalates as people roll up blankets and packs and drag themselves to the table, some bleary-eyed from hangovers, grumbling of sore backs, others irritatingly cheerful like Moku, whistling a jig.

The teamsters waste no time organizing the train. The bull punchers ready the ox teams, checking the wooden yokes around the beasts' necks. The skinners round up the mules and check the packs, and the family wagons fall in behind us and the other walking miners. There's no rain, but the wind is sharp. The earth feels hard underfoot, cold and pinched by frost. Snow's not far off. But it's a good day, for the wind is at our back. Moku's behind me with Zeke, humming to himself. Our bellies are full, and we're a day closer to the Cariboo.

The weather bites now. Snow's crawling down the mountainsides, and cold winds whip through the wagon train making canvasses flap. Drivers have to tie them down. We all bundle ourselves up. We stop when we reach Jackass. The entire train falls silent, while the men check and double check the wagons for safety. Every axle is inspected, every rein tightened and tested. We adjust our backpacks and blanket rolls. Yesterday's trek scared the Hawthorns, who fretted till we were through to Boston Bar. They're anxious about the wagons they bought in Yale and still don't know much about. Zeke and I help them tighten their leathers. Then we're off.

The climb up Jackass is steep, steeper than we imagined. Again, we hug the mountainside. I don't look at the roiling river below but keep my eyes on the road before me, carefully placing my feet on the stony ground, balancing my backpack and bedroll, and breathing deeply. Moku and Zeke do the same, and we three hold our pace behind the Hawthorns' wagons while one miner after another stops and falls behind us to rest. Up and on we go endlessly it seems, calves knotting, backs straining. My chest feels like it's being pressed against a stone wall. Kimo has a pain in his side and Zeke is in a world of his own, staring at his feet, plodding unsteadily forward. Then one of Hawthorn's wagons bogs down, and the teamsters rush to cut poles to try and pry its wheels out of the rut. It's not easy, for there's little room to move around on the road. The noise is deafening with men shouting and animals bawling. Zeke and Moku and I help but it's hard to keep feet planted with loose dirt and pebbles shifting beneath them. Then some unholy screaming reaches us from along the line.

"Mule's down," someone screeches, and there's a beast down on his forelegs, slipping and sliding toward the cliff edge. Men move out of its way as fast as they can, gingerly, but one wrong move and they'd be in the canyon too, so they shift with care, high stepping in some exaggerated exotic polka. One mule's already gone down, and he's hauling the other on the line after him. The frightened beast is braying but he's strangling, scraping his bleeding forelegs bare on the ground in an effort to hold on, grinding them through to the white bone. One of the skinners leaps to cut the mule's pack lines. The beast's packs heave and tip, the weight humps him forward and suddenly he's gone, screaming pitifully into the canyon. The other mules bray with fright but their handlers move quickly to grab Bessie, the lead white mare. White mares always lead the trains, for good luck. The skinners fight frantically to calm the agitated mules, and one of them gets kicked in the face for his trouble. His nose looks like a mashed potato, and his front teeth are knocked out top and bottom, but he picks himself up and spits, wipes the blood from his face and gets about his business. The skinners climb on the backs of the mules, to coax them forward again. I wouldn't be a skinner on Jackass for all the gold in the Cariboo.

We break another two pine poles but finally pry the stuck wagon wheel from its rut, and the train continues to climb up Jackass. It's a silent climb now, each step a test of endurance, each man breathing hard, thinking his own thoughts. Each man wondering whose life savings went over the canyon. And finally we're over Jackass, with the worst behind us.

A mile or two along the road, we stop at the roadhouse. People are in a good mood despite their exhaustion. No one died on Jackass. Two mules lost and some packs, that's all, so the teamsters are happy enough. The rest of us are ecstatic. The mood carries over into the roadhouse, where the food's not so good but whiskey flows freely, and there's singing and even some dancing, with the hurdy gurdy girls strutting their stuff, no charge.

The wagon train is heading for the Forks next — they call it Lytton, now — at the junction of the Fraser and the Thompson rivers. Then we'll head for Clinton, and beyond. Word is they've finished the road as far as Soda Creek, and soon they'll be cutting it through to Quesnelle and then east to the new mining towns. But the new town of Clinton is where the great Interior plateau is supposed to begin. It's hard to tell exactly, because there's not much mapped about the land yet, and people go on hearsay, with news passed miner to miner. If you can read, you can gather news of discoveries and place names from the newspaper that comes out of Victoria, but on the move it's hard to find a copy that isn't out of date.

The great plateau is called the Cariboo, after the herds of brown animals the size of small elk that roam the woodlands. It stretches from east of the Fraser to the Cariboo Mountains and from Clinton north to Quesnelle and beyond. And it's here men have come chasing dreams, trekking through the unknown to the creeks in search for gold.

It's a feeling I don't like much, not knowing exactly where we're going after we reach the plateau. Nothing's certain. Still, this whole wagon train is about taking chances. I see Morning Bird heading our way. She's taking her chances, too, I reckon, for what's ahead for her can be no worse than what's behind her. She's been to the water barrels in the Barnard's Express freight wagons again, toting a bucket back to her German family.

"Bad luck, they lose mules," she stops to say.

"How's your sick woman?" I ask.

"Scared. Children are good. I like. You need help?" Same question she asks every day. I give her the same answer.

"Thanks, but we're fine."

"I wish she'd quit wanting to tend us," I say to Zeke when she walks away. I figure she's grateful to us for freeing her, but after taking that bullet in Yale while she was with us — a bullet possibly meant for me — she owes us nothing.

"She still feels a slave, even if'n she gits paid for the job she's doin'. Goin' take a while 'fore she feels different."

I watch her back as she returns to the Germans' wagon, carefully picking her way across the rocky path. She has a heavy wool wrap round her shoulders to cut the cold but somehow she looks smaller in her European dress. It's grey cotton, calf-length and tied at the waist. Where would she get the money to buy a dress like that, I wonder? Maybe the Kwantlen paid her for arranging the canoe transaction. More likely the Germans gave her it. Her shoulder must be sore still, and carrying that bucket won't help.

"Seen her belly?" Zeke says. "Swolled up. Baby comin'."

"I missed that. Her husband's been dead since last winter so it can't be his," I speculate.

"Don't 'spect she'd have a say in who got her."

Slaves can be bought, given or gambled away, so anyone could've fathered her child. Her husband's brother, I wonder? The old man? We're still watching her when a miner appears between the Hawthorns' wagons and tugs on her elbow. He's a big, bearded man, wearing a Hudson's Bay red and black checkered shirt and high boots. She draws her arm sharply away. I can't hear their conversation, but she's shaking her head, jerking away from him. "No!"

Moku says "Do you want to deal with this, *aikane*, or will I?" But I'm already on my feet and striding the distance between us. The miner is dark complexioned and flabby, with his belly protruding over his pants. A winter digging in the Cariboo might do him good. His brown eyes are bloodshot. He has wide nostrils and a grey droopy moustache. I grab his shoulder.

"The woman says no."

"She's Indian," he counters, breathing whiskey.

"She still says no."

"What business is it of yours?"

"I'm making it mine."

Above the grey whiskers, his eyes narrow. Then they widen with a blaze of anger and he comes charging at me, mouth spewing curses. But I learned early how to fight — say nothing, make your opponent feel some pain and get out fast. When someone won't listen, hurting can make them suddenly hear better, and they soon get the message. Still, his reflexes are quick and he swings wild and lands some hard punches before I drive my fist into his solar plexus and that's the end of it. He drops to the dirt, then finds his breath and staggers to his feet mumbling. He stumbles away trailing whiskey fumes.

"Thank you, Kanaka." Her voice is small, quiet.

"He won't bother you again." I lick a spit of blood off my lip.

She nods and walks away. Even with the weight of the bucket she holds her head high, moving across the landscape placing one foot in front of the other with Indian ease. Natives know the earth. They feel the land. That's something Rose did. Morning Bird moves over the landscape the same way, as if it's part of her, placing her feet lightly on the earth, and doesn't spill a drop.

A little later we return to the roadhouse. We eat inside, but it's noisy and full of smoke. When a gun goes off outside, men pile through the doorway to see what's happening. A fight's taking place and men are shouting, fueled by the roadhouse whiskey and weariness. The freight men won't stand for trouble on their train, and set out to find the culprit when yet another shot rings out. This time a bullet whirrs past us so close Moku and I can feel the draft, entering the timber of the stair post with a muffled thunk, bare inches from where we're standing. The shock numbs us for a second.

"*Auwé!*" Moku touches the timber gingerly, at the bullet's entry hole. "You awright?"

I don't take time to answer. That first shot came from the fighting miners, but the post shot came from beyond the tree line where the cleared roadway meets the wilderness. I tear through the bushes into the trees. The wagon master comes running along with Moku and Zeke, weaving through the trees and bushes till we run out of breath.

"They got away," Zeke gasps. The wagon master continues to scout around.

"Maybe it was the miner who pestered Morning Bird earlier," Moku pants. We check the roadhouse, and find him reeking of whiskey fumes, snoring in a bunk in the men's quarters.

"How long's he been sleeping?" I ask the man in the next bunk.

"About an hour." So it wasn't him.

The freight men are peeved. They don't approve of guns going off at their roadhouse stops.

"Indians," the wagon master says when he and his men stomp back into the roadhouse. "Something's got 'em riled. We seen 'em slinking through the trees. They won't be back now night is falling. But when we move out tomorrow, stay in your groups, don't lag behind, and keep your eyes and ears open."

The miners are edgy. The women are scared. We take to our bunks. My head's reeling. Indians! I'm actually relieved. I was beginning to suspect Ahuhu! Wrong thinking can sure take over when your adrenalin's running high.

We'll need to keep a sharp lookout from here on. I can't feel the deep anger towards the natives that some do, though. Their land is being invaded, and here am I, one of the invaders. But I won't be a target for their revenge and I intend to keep my scalp intact. I think back to Oahu, that tiny gem in the blue Pacific, and how the *haolé* tide swept our islands. Here, there are great mountains, rivers, endless skies set in a land vast beyond imagining, with room for many people. I can't fault the natives for resisting, but think if they continue the Indian Wars they are postponing the inevitable, for, as in Hawaii, there will be no stopping the *haolé* tide sweeping this land.

We need sleep to get through what's ahead, so I order my tumbling thoughts to cease. My bunkmates are still talking about today's trek. On the wagon road, a line of dejected miners had passed us returning south.

"If strong men like that turn back, what chance do we have?" a European voice whines in the dark. I can't tell if he's Italian, French or Spanish. His English is good

"Should've thought of that in Yale," another answers abruptly, "and saved yourself a heap of money."

"Give up before you even start digging?" a derisive voice cuts in. "Fine poke of gold that'll fetch." His contempt ends the discussion.

The European's only voicing doubts we all have. But doubts can hobble you if you let them take root, so I don't give them space. Our goal remains: to reach the Cariboo. And the goldfields demand a stiff spine.

Next stop is the Forks. We're a day closer. And still alive.

chapter nine

I'M DREAMING. I'M IN Hawaii and it's hot. Sweat stings my eyes and salt crusts my lips, and the tropical air feels thick as morning porridge, with no cooling breeze to soothe the skin. The world is silent. Even the birds are hushed, hiding in the shade of nests high in the palms. Only the sea makes a sound, shushing up the beach urgently, as if to relay a message, but the words are too low to comprehend, so even half asleep, I know I've been away too long.

I wake shivering in a crumpled blanket on the cold wood floor. Men are up already, stomping around the room for warmth. I join Moku and Zeke to eat at the bench by the fire then head out to join the train. It's cold and we're layered in clothes. So is Morning Bird, wound up in a wool blanket on her way to the water wagon, with the youngest Hesse girl tagging along.

The child reminds me of Kami. I miss her but I have to stay

focused. It's all about the goldfields and moving forward, covering the distance each day and surviving.

"The three mining maps we copied in Langley are all different," I tell Moku. "Distances between creeks don't agree."

"That'll make for trouble when we prospect then," he says, shivering. We pore over the maps. They show the long Columbia Mountain range and the Cariboo Mountains that form the eastern edge of the Cariboo district, separating the plateau from the Rocky Mountain Trench. The Fraser curls round the top of the range, changes direction then heads south towards the coast. I point to the northern creeks.

"It's here they're finding the gold. But we have to figure out which creek to follow."

"We can hit the first saloon we reach," Moku says. "Men there will know where the latest strikes are."

The cold's getting worse. We're all bleary-eyed and sniffling. I think of heat now the way you do of food when you're hungry. But at least it's dry. A strong scent of sagebrush fills the air as we wind our way along the wagon road, bald eagles and ospreys soaring above and flurries of small birds heaving up in the air like dust in a storm. Elk, bighorn sheep and deer appear through the trees from time to time, working their way across the land as we do, though the animals likely know where they are bound and what waits for them. We've spotted cougars on the trail, and a late hibernating bear once, and at night wolves and coyotes howl. It's a wild and beautiful place we're passing through. Just damned cold.

It's a good thing we didn't paddle. There are eighteen rapids along this stretch. Counting them helps pass the time as we place one foot in front of the other in this interminable walk. The river roars and roils, tumbles and spurts like tea boiling in a kettle. The numbing cold is brutal. When I first came from Hawaii, I revelled in snow, in the first taste of it. I hauled on woollen sweaters and sat in it, licking the flakes with my tongue. But there's no joy in this snow, only hardship.

The rumble from the river deafens us. Men can paddle this stretch of water and live but others have drowned trying. No numbers, no names. You just see boats drifting broken and splintered in the calmer sections of the river.

And now Zeke's shouting, "There's the Forks!" and the little town appears ahead of us, round the river bend. Lytton it's called officially, after the British colonial secretary Sir Edward Bulwer Lytton, but people still call it the Forks. Or *Camchin*, its native name, meaning the meeting place. It sits on the bench lands above the confluence of the rivers, where the rushing green of the Thompson swirls into the silty brown of the Fraser. For a mile you can see the colours swirl around and through and into each other like cream in coffee, before merging into one.

"Don't look like much." Zeke frowns.

But Lytton is more or less what I imagined, another town like Yale, sprung up like a mushroom, new, all future and fake fronts. A grey winter light hovers over bare unpainted buildings. Clumps of dried grass and weeds spread along the muddy little streets but people walk about with purpose, as if they know what they're doing and why — grizzled men in sheepskin jackets and blanket coats, some wearing chaps, with oiled wool scarves tied over their hats and under whiskered chins. Not a high-necked white shirt in sight. Noises and smells fill the air — animals neighing and braying, men hollering from room windows and bar doorways. There's the chink-chink of a blacksmith's hammer and the plink-plonk of a piano from one of the bars. It sets Moku to whistling.

The hotels and rooming houses are full but we find a cheap room to share. The floor's never seen a broom and bits of black bugs wedge between the floorboard seams.

"Ah hope they's flies," Zeke stomps on one. "And not roaches."

We drop our gear, quit the room and head for the main street saloon to find out where the newest strikes are, for miners will talk. And talk. There's no secrets among them, unless they strike pay dirt and don't want the news to get out. We're lucky to find a table by the bar. The place is crowded, abuzz with a man at the counter drawing miners round him like bees to honey. Seems he's one of the party of gold seekers come to the Cariboo last year, having travelled overland across the continent. The hard men here can't conceive of such foolishness. The Overlanders' story was in the Victoria newspaper, the talk of every man heading for the goldfields.

"They come all the way from Upper Canada." The bearded barkeeper fills us in. "Three thousand miles, two hundred of them. With a pregnant woman and three children. What were they thinking?"

"O' gold. What else?" An old timer at the bar sidles over to our table. His back's bent. He's looking to sit. "They crossed the border, took the train and steamboat across America, re-crossed the border and met up in Fort Garry in June. Come over the Carlton Trail in two-wheeled Red River carts pulled by oxen, to Fort Ellice and Fort Carlton, then on to Fort Edmonton. That's near 900 miles along those old fur trails. With the worst still ahead, getting through the Rockies. Right?"

The man come overland nods. He's young, late twenties maybe. Thin, not real tall. A wiry type. He rests his elbows on the bar, sipping his beer slowly. He's got a look about him that reminds me of Zeke. It's his eyes. They're old. Like he's burdened with something.

"That's right." His voice is flat, expressionless, as if he's weary telling his story. "Half the wagon train left in Edmonton. They'd had enough. The rest of us drove horses and cows but had to set them free when the trails through the mountains died on us. We turned the cows into jerky in the end. It was a cruel trip through Blackfoot and Cree country. We ran out of food and water. We blazed trails, forded and rafted rivers. We traded with the Indians when we could, and hunted and gathered berries. Some days it was scorching hot, other days torrential rain churned up the dirt, and we'd get stuck feet-deep in mud. We ate what we could catch: skunk, crow, squirrels, after the jerky ran out. We rode, walked, swam and rafted our way to Jasper House and thought we'd seen the worst of it, but no. We still had to fight our way through the Rockies to Lillooet. Took us twice as long as we figured. Ended up at Tête Jaune Cache, half starved. We split up there. Some trekked into Kamloops. Others rafted down the Fraser. Some, like my friend James Carpenter, didn't make it."

"The one that wrote of his death afore it happened?" the barkeeper asks.

"One and the same," the young man says. The story has bounced around the Cariboo, and the young man swears it's true, that Carpenter wrote in his diary before he boarded the raft, *"was drowned running the canoe down. God help my dear wife . . ."*

The Overlander is no braggart, this young man with the distant eyes, nor is it the *tanglelegs* talking. I think his story proves again how the lust for gold can make men dispense with good judgment. He names names. Thomas McMicking led the group. Catherine Schubert delivered her child in Kamloops the day they arrived. What trials these desperate people went through. Yet I think as steel goes through fire, they must emerge as something new, something stronger than before, and I shake the hand of this foolish courageous soul come overland in such a way.

Sick of travelling, he says, many gave up the idea of prospecting and settled in the small towns where they arrived, or went south to Victoria, as he did. But now he's come back north.

"I'm heading for Barkerville to find gold before I settle for good," he says.

"Good luck. You've earned it," I say, though I know well enough luck isn't earned. It falls on the undeserving as much as the deserving. I just hope there's some left for us. Moku, Zeke and I, we could use it.

Lytton has a good feel to it. The bar's crowded, but there's no fighting. When the Overlander's news is exhausted, talk reverts to gold, where and how to find it and how to spend it. Since Billy Barker struck pay dirt, they say not five but ten thousand men have found their way north to William's Creek.

"Where are you headed?" the old timer at our table asks. "Need a horse or a mule — I got 'em."

"You trade horses?"

"Yes, sir. Tried mining. Got a broke back. Can't spade or fetch'n carry. But I got me enough gold to buy land and run horses on it. If you need a good mount, I'm seven miles along the Thompson." When he leaves, he whispers across the table "Forget Barkerville. Good claims are all took up. Take the trail out of 150 Mile House and head northeast to the Quesnelle. There's gold there for the picking."

We don't talk much after he leaves. Too much to think about. We head back to the hotel. Cold air hits our faces as we enter the room. A window opens to the adjacent rooftop and our backpacks lie open on the floor, contents strewn around the room.

"What the hell . . ." Moku charges off downstairs to find the clerk. Zeke and I take inventory.

"One shirt and a pair o' ma pants are gone," Zeke says.

"My spare boots are missing." I'm mad. They cost me plenty.

The clerk returns with Moku, points to the window and says we should've kept it shut. I feel like swiping him. Zeke strides from the room without a word and Moku snaps at the clerk, "We left it shut. What kind of hotel are you running?"

"The town's full of hungry men heading south. They'll steal the shirt off your back and trade it for food or liquor." He shrugs, acts bored. "Happens every day."

"Not to us it doesn't." Moku jabs him on the shoulder for emphasis and the man scuttles along the hall like a frightened beetle. An hour later Zeke walks through the door.

"Found a miner wearin' your boots outside the saloon," he says. "You got to see the constable. He says you need to sign a report to git them back."

"He could've just taken your statement," I point out.

"Ahm black," Zeke says.

"That makes no difference."

"It always makes a difference," he sighs. His mind is set in stone in that regard so I figure something in his life has made him leery of the law. I go with him to find the constable. It seems Zeke set about the thief after recognizing my boots, and was in the process of hauling them off the man's feet when the constable spotted them outside the saloon, where he'd been rounding up some brawlers. The thief's being held, pending charges.

The constable's sitting on a chair outside the flap of a white tent pitched on a green patch at the end of the storefronts on Main Street. Turns out the tent is the courthouse and it's in recess, so the constable has time to write up the charge for me to sign. After discussing Zeke's lost shirt and pants, he makes out a charge for Zeke to sign as well. Zeke makes his mark and I witness it.

"Kin you read it to me?" He's anxious, wanting to be sure it's recorded properly. It makes me wonder again what kind of law he's used to. The constable adds our two charges to his list, stands and opens the tent flap for us to go inside. A group of men are sitting at the far end of the tent beside a rough pine table. Zeke's antsy. His eyes dart all over the place, and he starts cracking his knuckles. He's not happy being here, but I suppose once the constable got involved, there was no avoiding it, unless we just cleared out and didn't lay charges. But boots and clothing are no small things here in the Cariboo and we need to get them back.

Then Judge Begbie strides long-legged into the tent in a great hurry, black robes flapping in the breeze, dressed as if he's in a court in Victoria. You could've knocked me down with a feather. They say he bangs his gavel in all kinds of unlikely places, holding court in cabins, hotels and outside beneath trees.

After he sits down at the table, he quickly settles a property dispute between two men, brothers quarrelling over their inheritance, then runs through the charges laid against the bar brawlers, fining them for disorderly conduct and ordering them to pay restitution for the property destroyed in the bar. He sentences a man for three years to a chain gang working on the roads, as punishment for stealing gold dust from his employer's claim. Then the constable reads out my charge and Zeke's charge together and calls Josef Manheim, the alleged thief, to stand before the judge.

The man is blond and slightly built. He has a hungry look about him, and is dressed in tatters. It's hard not to feel sorry for him. When he takes his oath he sounds European — German, I suspect. Zeke and I are called to rise also. Zeke's nervous, but stands tall. The judge hears the charges, then asks the constable to list again the items allegedly stolen.

"One pair of Hudson's Bay boots size 14, one grey shirt and one pair of men's work pants, stolen from the victims' backpacks in the hotel."

"And you, Mr. Kanui, have identified these boots as belonging to you, and accuse this man of stealing them?"

"Yes, Your Worship."

"What proof do you have they belong to you?"

"Well, they're at least four sizes too big for *him*," I say. Manheim is maybe five feet six inches tall at a stretch, with feet size 8 or 9. Someone snickers. The judge bangs his gavel for order.

"The left toe has an inch long mark from a missed axe cut," I tell him. "The other toe is fine, like new. And I wrote my initials under the tongue of each boot, Your Worship."

"Constable, check those boots." Manheim slowly unties the laces and slides the boots off.

"They're initialled, both of them. K.M.K. under each tongue, Your Worship."

"Guilty as charged!" Judge Begbie bellows. "Despicable. Small stealing leads to bigger stealing! Boots one day, gold pokes the next. Constable, return those boots to Mr. Kanui. Now Mr. Manheim, do you have this man Browne's missing clothes?"

"No, sir."

"Do you understand what perjury is, Mr. Manheim? May I remind you you're under oath? That this is a courthouse, and I can give the constable here authority to search your belongings?"

Manheim mumbles into his chin, then admits he has Zeke's clothing.

"If you hadn't lied, Mr. Manheim, you might be walking out with a fine. But you're going to jail for a month, not just for theft, but for barefaced lying in my court. Make this a lesson learned. Never, ever, lie in my courtroom, sir. Constable, retrieve those items for Mr. Browne." He bangs his gavel. "Case closed."

Zeke's happy, surprised his being black didn't influence the judge.

"You were the victim here," I remind him. "What did you expect?" I knew he'd get justice. Begbie's known for fair treatment. Doesn't matter if you're Chinese, native or white. The Haranguing Judge, some men call him, for he tends to scold the guilty, as he did Mr. Manheim. Maybe that's how he got the name the Hanging Judge, it just being easier to say. I'm thinking it's probably a good thing the German's going to jail. At least he'll get fed there, and come out healthier than he looks going in. Maybe the judge figured that too. At any rate, justice is served and we're happy. We head for the saloon to celebrate. We buy two whiskeys and, when we leave, we bump into the judge speaking with the constable on the plank boardwalk outside the saloon. The judge is smoking a cigar. The constable holds out Zeke's shirt and pants.

"Yours, I believe, Mr. Browne."

The judge extends his hand to Zeke. "Wear them in good health, sir." I doubt that anyone's called Zeke "sir" before. He preens.

"Heading to the goldfields, are you?" the judge asks. He speaks with a crisp, proper English accent. It suits him, matching his crisp British exterior and air of authority. I don't know if he's being condescending. I think not. He looks us straight in the eye, and seems genuinely interested.

"Yes, Your Worship. Thanks for finding in our favour. I remember seeing you when I worked at the fort, the day Mr. Douglas swore you in."

"Ah, yes. That was a wet day for such an auspicious occasion," he says. "You must excuse us, though. The constable and I have an appointment. Good luck finding your gold, gentlemen."

The two head down the boardwalk to a mule train just halted at the road's end. The judge picks up a heavy trunk from the packer. The constable has to help him lift it. The packer is the Frenchman, Jean Caux, "Cataline," a fine looking man, tall, with broad shoulders and a barrel chest. His hair is long and wavy, and he sports a full beard. I read a poster about his packing service in Yale. He supplies the mining camps and is probably the most popular man in the Cariboo because he never fails to deliver. He's wearing a handkerchief around his neck and a long open frock coat, a boiled white shirt, wool pants and riding boots. Zeke admires his wide-brimmed hat.

"You can buy one when we hit pay dirt," I say. He could never afford one like that right now. The judge is busy pumping Cataline's hand, grinning widely. Looks like they're old friends, the judge and the packer. That's one thing I've noticed about the Cariboo; it levels people. The goldfields have drawn so many different kinds of people here, there's such a mix of miners and natives and shopkeepers, all doing business together, and no one cares what colour your skin is or where you come from.

When we return to our hotel, the Overlander is signing in at the desk. We warn him to lock his door and windows as there are thieves about. I wouldn't want him to run into any more bad luck than he has already. We accompany him upstairs and say goodnight. Moku's already asleep. I toss and turn, my mind returning to those brave, foolish Overlanders, and that exhausted soul, the man Carpenter, foretelling his own death before he rafted downriver. And I think, in this and other ways, the Cariboo and the hunt for gold has killed more good men than enough, and I pray to whichever god is listening, that if we must die a sudden brutal death, we never know the day or way it'll happen.

chapter ten

NEXT MORNING THE WAGON train sets out for Cut Off Valley, "The Junction" at 47 Mile House. It's called Clinton now, after some English duke. I find it confusing that there's two Mile Zeros now, from both Lillooet and Yale. With the wagon road built, roadhouses are known by the mileage from Yale to Clinton. After Clinton, they count the mileage as before, from Lillooet. None of the roadhouses beyond Clinton have changed their names. So 129 Mile House, from Yale, is just a few miles south of 47 Mile House. The one thing you can always count on in this place is change.

Morning Bird tells us it's still Secwepemc territory here. The Secwepemc around Fort Kamloops are friendly, but that's no guarantee they're friendly up here. We leave Lytton and the Fraser, joining the men walking beside the mules, and head east along the clay benches of the Thompson, through acres of high land covered in Jack pines. We're two miles along the road when we hear a hoarse cry: "Indians! Up on the bench lands."

"There's twelve," Zeke squints and points north. "Three mounted and the rest standin'." I see them, feet apart, holding rifles. One lifts his weapon and pumps his arm fiercely.

"They won't harm us," Morning Bird assures the Hesse family. "No war paint." The train moves along and we're all on edge, but she's right. There are more of us, armed, and the Indians won't do anything against such odds. We're not about to let our guard down, though. We have a long way to go.

The wagon road moves overland now and won't meet the Fraser till Soda Creek, beyond our stop at 150 Mile. It's growing colder every day and we've heaped on more clothing. We have good boots but envy the long waterproof coat the wagon master wears. Winter's cruel up here. No wonder so many leave. We continue to pass them on the road: pale, thin grey ghosts who've taken all the hardship they can take, scraps of people, blown off the road of life from chasing after gold.

"Their leaving means more room at the diggings for the likes of us, willing to winter through," Moku says. His teeth chitter with the cold, but he can see the upside of this sad stream of humanity moving south.

"If'n we survive," Zeke adds the reality.

It's fifteen cold hard miles to the next roadhouse. A stage is tied up there already, beside winter sleighs, in case it's too cold for the stage to run. But they figure there's another week or two before winter forces the changeover, so they exchange horses as usual. The handlers treat their horses well, brushing coats till they shine, braiding tails. We leave the stage men to their chores, and make our way up the roadhouse steps. No one wants to camp outside now. Too wild, too raw, too cold. We join the scramble for benches near the fire.

A hot meal, a night's sleep and we head out for the junction of the Nicola and Thompson rivers, and find a boatman named Cook to ferry us across the Thompson. It's done in stages, and takes time. Talk is some man named Spence is planning to build a bridge here soon for those wanting to cross faster. *Haolés* are always in a hurry. While we wait our turn, Morning Bird steps off the Hesse wagon. She looks thin and pale and I watch her flex her shoulders back and it hits me. Her stomach's flat. Indian women, like the women of Hawaii, know the value of herbs. I feel for her, whether she lost the child or brought it about. Both require courage.

I'm uneasy as she approaches. I feel ashamed now of our behaviour in Yale. I regret how callous we were sending her on her way, judging her a burden after she took that bullet. She's a fine looking woman, with a dignified, calm strength about her. Moku and Zeke scramble to greet her, and she tells us that her German bought land north of Clinton, sight unseen, to raise horses on the say-so of friends, it being a lush valley with bunch grass in summer as high as your waist.

That may be so, but summer seems a long way off while this cold is eating into us. After we finally cross on the raft ferry, we're back on the trail, with its muddy ruts gone hard, scrunching up cold beneath our boots. Snow's coming down on and off, and it's a day's hard walk to Ashcroft Manor to overnight, then another hard day's walk to Clinton. It's much like Lytton when we get there: another town sprung up quick as a tuft of grass, muddy Main Street, pine shacks and false fronts, living on dreams, surrounded by steep hills and soaring pines.

"Folks be leavin' us here." Zeke taps my shoulder. The Hawthorn family wagons are lined up one behind the other, piano intact as far as I can tell. We shake their hands and wish them well. Morning Bird and the German family draw their wagon alongside, and call out their goodbyes. Nelson Hawthorn leans across the space between their wagons and says something to Morning Bird. He's taken a liking to her. I've watched him at the mile houses, whispering in her ear, hovering around her offering coffee or blankets. She leans towards him to catch his words, then laughs and settles herself back on the bench beside Mrs. Hesse. The Hesses are staying with the train till the next roadhouse.

Moku hollers, "Good luck!" as the Hawthorn wagons pull away. Mrs. Hawthorn under her heap of blankets looks teary-eyed and sad, and a little afraid. Zeke waves and I tip my hat as their wagons lurch past, flapping canvasses, wheels grinding up snow-covered dirt along the main road then veering off east of town. As they disappear over the horizon, powdery snow starts to fall again and I worry about this genteel English family being a poor fit for such a harsh place. Land will make or break you. I hope they make it, piano and all.

We head for the saloon, for news of the diggings. We've barely finished our first whiskey when a hand taps my shoulder.

"*Mes amis! Mon Dieu!* I'm sorry you see me like this." The rasping voice belongs to Guy Leclerc. The wiry, balding Canadien clasps Moku and me like long lost brothers. He's so thin, I don't hug him hard, in case his bony shoulders break. A voyageur, he worked with us at the fort years ago but we hardly recognize him, he looks so old. Mottled, wrinkled skin stretches across his bony cheeks. His jaws are clapped in, and his beard, which hasn't seen a razor in months, reaches mid-chest. His small eyes are sad and dark as currants beneath thin eyebrows. He would sing and dance jigs after downing the fort's rum, but there's no joy in the man now. Fatigue oozes from his pores. He's looking for a Swede whose claim is near his, he says, but he can't find him.

"Amundsen comes to Clinton to visit a lady friend, spends a few days here in the saloon, then comes back when he feels like it but he's a good man, an' my friend. I want 'im to know I'm leaving but can't find 'im." Leclerc orders a whiskey. He's quitting his claim, he says, because he's sick and can't recover enough strength to work it. He has blisters on both hands and an axe cut that's gone septic on his right wrist.

"You git much gold out yo' claim?" Zeke wants to know.

"Enough to fill a few pokes. I 'ad a partner and we worked together, but 'e left two months ago an' it's too hard for one man to work."

"Then anybody kin pick it up," Zeke says. "If'n a claim's not worked for seventy-two hours, it's officially abandoned. Jest need to git a gold commissioner to register it. You giving it up for good?"

"*Oui*. Never will I come back. Never. Amundsen might want it but he's not here and I can't wait around to tell him." He shrugs. "It's yours if you want it."

We're struck dumb for a moment.

"Where are you going?" he wants to know. "Do you 'ave a creek in mind?"

"No. We're thinking Barkerville eventually, anywhere around that area."

"William's Creek is all staked out. All you'll get now in Barkerville is a job digging for somebody else."

We don't need to think twice. Luck's a capricious thing, never coming when you hope for it, but appearing when you least expect it, and ours has come in the unlikely form of the voyageur Guy Leclerc. We can take over where he left off. And if it doesn't pan out, we can always move farther north. We grin like fools and decide we will head to the nearest gold commissioner with a letter from Guy quitting his claim, and one from us claiming it. I write the note for Guy and he signs it.

We are jubilant. But we need to move fast in case some other miner sees it's abandoned and gets the same idea. Guy draws us a rough map. Beaver Creek flows into the Quesnelle, about halfway between

Quesnelle Mouth at the junction with the Fraser, and Quesnelle Forks, sixty miles upstream by Quesnelle Lake. Guy marks the position and number of his claim for us.

"I 'ave left tools an' a stack of wood. Claim number is writ clear on the pegs. Der's good diggings nearby. A German, named Wouk, he takes out a hundred dollars one day just along the creek."

"We'll have to do this right," I tell Moku and Zeke. "We need to pick a name for ourselves, and spell out that it's a company owned by the three of us, to make it legal and proper. We'll register it with the gold commissioner and apply for Guy's abandoned claim."

Right there in the saloon we decide on a company name and hold a vote to name the officers. I'm to be president, Moku vice-president, and Zeke secretary of the Lucky Three Mining Company, formed to search for gold in the Cariboo which, if found, will be shared equally by the three partners. Signed by me, Kimo Maka Kanui. Moku makes his mark, and Zeke his, all witnessed by Guy Leclerc. We offer him money for the claim, but he declines.

"*Non.* I was leaving anyway. You may as well 'ave it. I see you back in Langley one day; you can buy me a drink." We settle on some dollars for the wood he's left behind, shake hands and Guy takes his leave.

"Boil some water," Zeke tells him, "an' soak yore wrist and tie a sugar poultice on it till you find yo'self a doctor." Zeke's got all kinds of remedies in that head of his.

We overnight at the Clinton Hotel then head out with the wagon train next day for 70 Mile, twenty-three miles north. We tramp in silence, conserving energy, for it's uphill this stretch. The iron cold bites ears and noses and makes breathing hard. I'm thinking we need to get to the creek and settle quickly, that we should've left sooner after all. We'll need shelter before digging begins, for our tents won't do.

This is reinforced when we reach 70 Mile. The roadhouse is so crowded, with every inch of bed and floor space taken up, that we're forced to pitch our tents outside. It's bitterly cold and snow's falling in flurries, but we're so exhausted we sink into sleep anyway. Morning brings a bitter surprise.

"Kimo! Moku! Git up! Our bundles are gone!" Zeke's standing over us with his rifle in hand. He's always up first, relieving himself. "We's in trouble."

We scramble to our feet, fighting our way up from sleep.

"The bundles?" I mumble.

"Gone! Ours, and other folks'." The packs were inside our tent at our feet. How could someone have come in so silently and taken our gear without us knowing? Lucky we slept with our rifles in our bedrolls or they'd be gone too. We step outside, and find irate miners milling around. And Morning Bird, who's been to the Barnard's Express wagon for drinking water already.

"They left boot prints in the snow," one of the miners says.

"They's moccasin tracks, not boots," Zeke points out. He's right. And they're fresh. "They're not long gone. We kin catch them," he says.

"Thieving bastards!"

"Let's teach them a lesson!"

Morning Bird sets down her water pail. "I come. Maybe help find them. Talk trade. Get packs back."

"Trade with thieves?"

"No bloody way!"

"I want my gear back!"

"We need to teach 'em a lesson, that's what we have to do."

I speak over the angry voices. "Arguing just wastes time. How many packs are missing? Eight? There's three of us. We need one of you to come with us. The rest, stay here and decamp. A group of noisy miners chasing through the trees won't get our packs back. It'll just tell them we're coming. Morning Bird, we accept your offer. You know the people. That might help."

The wagon train is due to leave in just three hours, so we've no time to waste. We set out: Zeke, Moku, Morning Bird, myself and one of the miners, an American from Tennessee. If Morning Bird thinks she can be useful, she's likely right. We follow the tracks into the woods. I figure they took the bundles one by one from the tents and stashed them in a heap, for we find a bare circle of ground and from that circle, marks of packs being dragged.

"Not far," Morning Bird says. "Only three braves."

"There must be more. There's eight bundles missing." I still don't know how they could sneak in and open and close four tents so silently, with no one hearing a sound.

"Only three," she says again. We move through the trees silently, listening for breaking twigs or the sounds of bundles but there's no sound, except for the morning chirping of birds. I suddenly spot our bundles, heaped up in a pile against the trunk of a tall pine.

"There they are," I start to say, when I hear the small, clear, deadly *click*. I swing towards the sound to find a brave staring back at me through rifle sights, barely three feet away. *Click!* A smaller brave faces Moku. *Click!* Another faces the American miner. Zeke and Morning Bird can do nothing, or we three will see a bullet. We hadn't heard them. Not a whisper, not a breath, not a footfall.

One of the braves barks an order. He is tall for an Indian, about six feet, and dressed in deerskin. He's thin and hungry looking. Morning Bird holds out her hands showing she has no weapon. "Lay down your rifle," she tells Zeke. He grips it fiercely, then slowly drops it to the forest floor.

"*Midlight!*" the brave shouts.

Morning Bird squats on the ground. "He say sit." Moku looks at me, and then to Zeke and the American and we slowly scrunch to the ground. "He scared," Morning Bird says. He doesn't look scared to me. He looks angry. But he's not wearing war paint. A good sign.

Morning Bird speaks to him softly mostly in Halq'emeylem, with some Chinook thrown in, so I know they don't speak the same dialect. I hear the word *Q'eyts'i*, and *Oihes*. He continues to shout angrily while she responds in quiet, low tones. The other two braves flank us as we sit, rifles pointed at our heads, but they're young, and distracted by their leader's loud talk. When he speaks, they nod in agreement. They're just boys, full of the passion of youth.

Moku eyes me. He sees it too. I nod and we pounce together. Our ancestors were warriors, and we won't retreat from a challenge by these young men. I grab the barrel of the rifle of the brave nearest me and yank it upwards, kneeing him hard in the groin. Moku has the short brave's rifle in hand now, and with a heavy smack, knocks the young Indian to the ground. In the scramble, amidst screams and yelling, Zeke jumps to his feet and reclaims his rifle, aiming it now at the leader. The American too retrieves his revolver. Zeke and the braves' leader glare at each other, eye to eye, then the young Indian slowly lowers his rifle. Morning Bird remains seated. "We talk now," she says.

Moku looks at me wide-eyed. Zeke shakes his head. I don't know what she's doing. But I trust her.

"We should get the hell out of here!" the American says.

"Sit!" I haul him down with me to the ground. The three Indians squat beside each other facing us, looking ill at ease. "Morning Bird, ask them if they shot at the pack train at the roadhouse after Jackass."

She speaks with the leader, then sits quietly nodding. "Yes," she says. "They're Tsilhqot'in. They're afraid for their land — like the tribes of the south. Some miners treat them badly, and take their women. They move the native fishing racks, so the natives can't dry their fish for winter, and lose their food supply. They worry because they've lost fathers, mothers, brothers and sisters to smallpox. They think the pack trains will bring back the disease. They want to stop them coming."

"So they rob them, hoping they will stay away?"

"Yes. There say there are too many white men now."

"Tell them I'm sorry about the disease. My own father died from the pox when I was a boy. I understand their sorrow. But we bring no smallpox in our train. None. Tell him too that we are not all white men on this train. I am *Oihe*."

I roll up my sleeve. "See?" Moku rolls up his sleeve as well. Zeke doesn't have to. The Indian can't take his eyes off him.

"Tell him we understand his fear, but this is a big land, and there is room for many people, for all to live in peace with each other." I could tell him the white men have come to stay, that there are as many of them as blades of grass in the field, and they will keep coming as sure as the sun shines and the rain falls. But this is not what he wants to hear.

"Tell him we are passing through, going north, to find gold and will go away again. Tell him if they're hungry, we can spare them some food." The leader exchanges glances with the other Indians. I quickly root around my pack for pemmican and dried berries and find some ship's biscuits. I hand him the food. He bites into the ship's biscuit and spits it out. "Ugh!" Still, he shoves it, with the pemmican and berries, into a deerskin pouch tied round his waist. The thing reminds me of MacKay's sporran. He waves his right hand in the air then turns it towards us, palm up. Natives never point with the finger, this being unspeakably rude.

"He says if war comes to the Tsilhqot'in, you best return south quickly. Their chief, Alexis, is for peace, but others, like 'We do not know his name,' are ready to make war."

"He doesn't know whose name?"

"Klatsassin. It means 'we do not know his name.'"

Native logic is sometimes beyond me. The three Indians rise to their feet, and point to their rifles. I hesitate. I don't know if I trust them. Morning Bird raises an eyebrow ever so slightly, so I nod. Moku and Zeke return the men's rifles, while the leader picks his up off the ground. In a flash they are gone, into the trees soundlessly. We don't see the direction they take. Around us are the sounds of the forest, wind in the trees and chirping birds. And our packs, still heaped against the giant pine.

Moku volunteers to stay with the bundles, while Morning Bird, Zeke, the American and I tote what we can back to the roadhouse. The miners missing their packs return for their stolen gear and we have time to eat and decamp before the train has to leave. The man from Tennessee comes by.

"Thanks for helping me get back my gear. I could never afford to replace it. I'd have had to return south, trekking back on my own."

"We were lucky," I tell him.

"I suppose the Indians have a right to be angry. Still, they don't need to go about thieving, scalping and shooting at civilized people."

"True," I agree. I feel the natives' frustration. But robbing the pack trains to stop the white men coming won't work. That'll just result in more armed security.

I'm not a learned man, but I believe men can and do behave badly in uncertain times — men of every colour. Here, now, I see a great white wave swamping the native people, washing over their land, leaving them gasping for air, like fish out of water. This American speaks of civilized people, but the natives' environment and way of life is being ripped apart, outmatched by weapons and white know-how — roads and bridges are being thrown up on their lands, mountains are blasted apart, rivers are panned for gold, creeks dammed.

One civilization is tearing another, older one apart. I know how the natives must feel. How could I not? I am Kanaka.

The wagon train moves in numb procession, the bitter cold making us all wretched by the time we reach 100 Mile House. The teamsters call it Bridge Creek, and it's here the Hesse family is quitting the train to head west, to the ranchland Hesse has purchased sight unseen. The German sits up front on the box seat, with Morning Bird and the two girls beside him swaddled in great wool blankets. His sick wife is inside the wagon. The son must be inside with his mother. Morning Bird will have her hands full.

"Good luck!" Moku hollers and Zeke waves his hat in the air. Morning Bird lifts a hand in salute but I can't read her eyes. Like wind on a lake, her expression's here a moment then gone. I wave for them to wait, while I walk over to shake Hesse's hand.

"Good luck. I hope your wife feels better soon, Mr. Hesse. Take care of those little ones. Look after that shoulder, Morning Bird. Aloha!"

"Aloha?"

"It just means goodbye." It means of course, much more than that. "Take care of yourself," I add. I watch them ride away and disappear from view, and feel unsettled and apprehensive. I hope she'll make out all right.

We trek on, overnighting at 115 Mile, then veer northwest to Lac la Hache, named for an axe some prospector dropped and no one cares to rename it. It's a fine lake but the road's heavy going, crude and so rough on this stretch that the animals stumble and stagger. We overnight at 127 Mile — men call it Blue Tent Ranch, for that's how it started, though now it's made of wood — and next day we make the long trek to 141 Mile and stop. We can't think straight for the cold. Mind and bodies are numb. The roadhouse food and the heat from the fire put us to sleep instantly. The next day's trek is blessedly short, though, for we reach 150 Mile by early afternoon, and the place is immense. We feel like doing a jig. We're here. We made it. We're all in one piece. Everything's working to plan.

The roadhouse is a big two-storey log building with a store attached. Inside, near a large pot-belly stove, a shoulder-high stack of logs sits next to a huge fireplace that throws heat to the rafters. Men are eating, drinking, gambling and pushing coloured balls around on a table with long sticks — billiards, they call it. We know this game from Yale. We eat and drink and don't feel tired after only nine miles walking. In fact we are near light-headed with confidence now we've arrived. Moku can't stop whistling. Zeke pokes around outside then calls us to join him.

"Men heading south are sellin' tools out here. They want rid of them; they're cheap." We look, and find some rusty shovels lying around for the taking. To build a cabin, we buy a used crosscut saw and pick up an old froe for splitting roof shingles. Zeke adds an adze to our packs, to level logs for furniture.

It's here we must leave the wagon train to head out along the trail that cuts northeast to Quesnelle Forks, so I bargain for a big old mule from a departing miner, to pack our gear and purchases. The animal's name is Fouter, a Scots word, the man tells us, for an exasperating aimless muddler. I hope it's not prophetic. The animal has a torn right ear and sour breath that smells like wet grass. His forelock's thin, his mane coarse, but his tail is bushy and long. His grey-brown coat sports bald patches and he needs a good feed, but his almond-shaped eyes stare at me with the devotion of a puppy wanting fed.

"I'll take him," I say, and seal the deal. We tie him up alongside the wagon train's mules outside. His former owner left him with an old red wool blanket, so we won't have trouble finding him among the other mules in the morning. I sleep like a dead dog and don't want to move when Moku shakes me awake next morning. Since we'll cook for ourselves from here on, and likely end up thin as stalks, we eat all we can cram into our mouths at breakfast. After the wagon train heads out for Soda Creek, we check our maps.

"Bundle up and let's go." Zeke's testy, feeling the cold more than we do. He loops a wool scarf around his neck and over his hat. We do the same, pack our gear on Fouter and head out. We have to follow the same route as the wagon train for about fifteen miles, then we'll veer off northeast along the trail leading towards Quesnelle Forks. Now we're alone with only our thoughts and each other and the land blanketing us. The power of this place is overwhelming, for its rivers and great mountains and valleys dwarf men. You feel insignificant — an afterthought of whatever god created us. None of us speak. The silence seems too solemn, too pure for breaking.

Two hours from 150 Mile, we rest. Zeke builds a fire and boils water for tea. Moku heads for the trees to relieve himself and moments later we hear a sharp two-toned whistle. Zeke and I race towards the sound and find Moku squatting on his haunches beneath an overhanging pine.

"Corpse," he grimaces. What looks like a pile of rags is a dead miner set on the ground, back against the trunk of a tree. There's a note pinned to his chest. He's more bones than human and there's a dreadful stink coming out of him. I kneel and read the note.

Malcolm McGregor, born 1831, Fife, Scotland.
Broken leg. Dying in the wilderness.
Pray for my soul.

Some animal has gnawed at one of his legs and bone protrudes through the rotting flesh. The bone's cracked and split, no doubt to suck out the marrow, and most of his left foot is missing. Moku gags.

"Lawd! Bad luck hits here, youse on your own. No-one's gwan stop an' help no-how."

Men turning back speak of this, that there's little help in the wilderness, for people eking out an existence can't afford to give away even the smallest thing, or they themselves won't survive. But seeing this poor soul shocks us. We return to camp for shovels and try to dig a hole to bury the man McGregor under the pine, but the ground is too hard, so we cover him with gathered stones as best we can. The stink makes us nearly fetch up but eventually we pound a stake into the ground and scratch the man's name on it with a nail. We tie his shirt around the stake with his note attached. We'll report his death to the authorities next town we reach.

Zeke steps back, mumbling in that deep bass voice of his. In Hawaii, a man wouldn't die this way, alone in hunger and distress. But this is the Cariboo. I feel sad for the man. And his family. His parents have lost a son. Had he a wife? Or a child, perhaps? Are they still safe in their homeland, or did they come with him, left behind in some safe place while he pursued his dream here? How will they ever know what happened to him, to this son, to this husband, to this father? I think of my Kami and my heart contracts.

I squat on the ground beside Moku. We pay homage the Hawaiian way, chanting a funeral *mele* for the man so his soul will roam homeward across this vast land, over these mountains and over the seas. We stand, face west, and throw his name to the wind. I have nothing to offer but a plug of tobacco from my pocket. We break it over the pile of stones and head back to camp with Zeke wide-eyed and rattled, mumbling prayers to himself.

I brush the mule and let him forage for grass, digging through the snow with his hooves, while Moku cooks up peas and bacon and boils water for tea over the campfire.

"Kin a body git some coffee round here?" Zeke mutters.

"Why didn't you say sooner?" Moku says. He and I drink tea. "We'll take turns, tea one meal, coffee the next. How's that?"

"Jes fine." No one complains about meals. What the cook puts in front of us gets eaten, every morsel. That's understood. We eat in silence though, the dead man on our minds. I wonder again what's ahead. For a split second, I wish I'd never heard of the Cariboo, but it passes. We've made it this far. For Moku, the Negra and me, there's no turning back.

chapter eleven

WE HEAD OUT AGAIN along the trail. It's about four feet wide, well packed with a coating of snow over the hard ground. The spruce and Jack pine alongside have been hacked down by miners for fuel, shacks, flumes and other needs. Four Chinamen leading mules appear. We hear them talking to one another before we see them. They fall silent as we pass, yellow skin and pigtails, all smiles and bowing heads. They're wearing silver bracelets that jangle, Chinese loose tops with wool jackets over them, black pants and heavy boots. "Wah Lee" is stamped in black ink on all sides of the large wooden boxes slung over their mules, and they're heading back to 150 Mile House, come down the trail from Quesnelle. Their sturdy mules make scrawny Fouter look bad.

"Find gold?" Moku asks as they smile and bob their way along the trail.

"Find gold?" one repeats, bowing low. "Find gold? Good ruck."

"Smiles that wide mean they hit pay dirt," Moku mutters.

"Chinamen find gold where others don't," Zeke says.

It occurs to me that here we are, two Hawaiians and a Negraman meeting up with four Chinamen on a trail in the Cariboo, yet it doesn't feel the least bit strange. It's what happened in Hawaii. When *haolés* come, life changes forever with new people, new ways, being fetched up in their wake.

But now Oahu swamps me and I long for warmth and sun and blue skies. I close my eyes and pretend it's the old Hawaii, and I'm up in the high Koolaus. It's hot. The sun is setting out on the blue Pacific and a gentle wind breezes down the footpath leading to the sea. But then I picture foreign faces walking beneath the leafy palms, and my mind sees what the heart denies and I'm suddenly back in the cold Cariboo, on this trek to the Quesnelle, trailing this old mule. My nose is dripping, my fingers numb and walking's grown monotonous. We push one foot in front of the other. The wind whines endlessly and all a body can hear is the crunch-crunch of boots on crusted snow. They're sturdy, thank God: from the Hudson's Bay store, with iron heels and soles near an inch thick, full of round-headed nails and bought big, to wear with two pairs of wool socks to keep our feet warm.

We make it to Big Lake as dark falls, and pitch the tent. We sleep near each other for heat, rolled in extra blankets, taking turns to stoke the fire through the night. It's so cold, you worry when you take a piss that you'll be rooted to the ground till it thaws in spring. Morning brings more snow, and we're on the trail with Fouter at daybreak. I'm beginning to like the mangy beast. Fouter may be ugly but he's sure-footed even when piled high with provisions, and he keeps moving forward in spite of the icy air blowing in his face making his torn ear flap. Men say mules are stubborn but they're smarter than they get credit for. A horse now, he'll work till he drops. No mule will do that. He'll work hard for you and, if he balks, it's because he's trying to tell you that something's not right.

Miners pass us returning south — half-starved, broken men in ragged, tattered layers of clothing. One with no shoes has tied bits of sacking round his bleeding feet, and leaves a trail of red in his wake in the snow.

"Poor beggar has swapped his boots for scraps of food," Moku mutters. The man's face is shot with misery, and I wonder how far he can trek like this.

"I jes hope he don't end up propped agin a pine," Zeke says.

The land here is all mountains and forest, creeks and canyons. We plod on in cold silence to Beaver Lake, where there's a roadhouse.

"We can reach the cross-trail then get to the creek before dark, if we keep going," Moku says, and we're all so keen to get to the claim, we pass the roadhouse and plod on. At the cross-trail, we take the small fork west and after three hours, reach Beaver Creek. We follow the creek as the trail rises and falls and winds its way through countryside heaved up by diggings, waste piles of dirt and wood, flumes in various stages of disrepair, and mining debris. Claims have been pegged all along the creek. We don't see as many miners around as claims though. Maybe they've abandoned them. Or maybe the owners are hibernating. Every now and again, we pass a miner wintering over. Some are living in flimsy tents. Others have dug holes in the ground for shelter, and shoved bits of corrugated metal overhead for roofing. A few have put up windbreaks and rough shacks against the cold that grows more bitter each day.

"It's stupidity that's killing them," Moku says of the unprepared, but we feel sorry for their desperation. It's grown dark and we haven't reached Guy's claim after all, so we camp on the flat land off the trail. It's been snowing all day and the cold has slowed our progress. Moku builds a fire from bits of dried wood Zeke collects, while I unload Fouter. We cook up bacon and beans; Zeke's hot coffee pipes life into us. We rig the tent beneath and between some trees. Fouter finds his way around it for shelter too. The cold keeps us from sleeping well and when we wake next morning, Zeke's got something to say even before we exit the tent. All I can see are his eyes. Every inch of his face is hidden by layers of scarf that muffle his voice. He shifts his scarf away from his lips so I can hear.

"First, we build us a cabin. Then we dig. I ain't livin' in no hole in the ground." Moku and I aren't inclined to argue with him. Men are sleeping in pits barely big enough to hold a man. They crawl out to work their claims, cold and miserable and shaking the snow that fell overnight off their stiff bodies. It's lying a foot deep now, making it hard to walk. Old Fouter keeps his head down and plods along but the cold wind blasting his face has made pus seep from his left eye and it's stuck closed. Mid-morning we reach Guy's claim, about a mile from where the creek runs into the Quesnelle. Moku hunts for and locates the claim pegs while Zeke makes a fire and I unload the mule and tie and water him as close to the fire as he'll go without balking. I brew up some strong black tea, and after heat creeps into my bones, I let Fouter lap up the warm dregs from my tin cup. Then I use the left-over tea to wash the crusted pus out of his eye while it's snowing flakes the size of biscuits. I can't believe we've done it, that we're here, on our own claim, with a creek running by and gold maybe lying on the bottom just waiting to be picked up. But first things first.

"We need to file the claim before we can do anything. The nearest gold commissioner's at Quesnelle Forks. I'll go."

"No. I will," Moku says, before I draw another breath. "You two can set up camp." He was always a good trekker, faster than me.

"Zeke?"

"Suits me."

"Good. The day's only half gone. No point wasting time. I'll head out now."

After we eat, Moku hauls on his pack and sets out whistling. He'll follow the creek to the Quesnelle River, then head east to the Forks. He figures on covering a fair distance before dark as long as the snow holds off. Zeke hauls out the tools we bought at 150 Mile. We need to chop logs for a cabin. It won't be fun — the air's raw and it's icy underfoot. I hate this wretched cold the way only a soul from a hot clime can.

"Yore friend, the Frenchman, was never handy with tools." Zeke raps his knuckles against the lean-to, Guy's shelter on the flat above the creek. It's poorly built, and open at one side. Wind is whistling through it. "It's barely standin'."

I shove the wall with my fist, and the thing shudders sideways and near topples. The wooden floor boards beneath my feet feel soft with rot. Guy must've used old wood, leftovers maybe from an earlier miner.

"At least it's flat," Zeke says. "We kin pitch the tent inside for shelter while we's buildin'. First we need to replace the floor boards."

"Guy left some lumber. Let's check it out." We find two bundles of rough cedar boards two inches thick, twelve inches wide and twelve feet long.

"How'd they git here?"

"He said some Indian towed them from a sawmill near the Forks then hauled them in. We should look for him along the river, in case we need other supplies that he can bring in for us. Meantime there's a big cedar fallen by the creek, Zeke. Cut some three-foot blocks off it for making shingles, and I'll scout for poles for the framework."

I cut and peel eight poles before dark: four for corner supports, two for a door, and two for a window. Zeke thinks I'm crazy wanting a window.

"It'll be smoky if we need to cook indoors," I argue. "Not a glass window, not yet, but a wood frame panel that we can put up and down."

Zeke has trouble cutting the cedar rounds so I take over the saw while he warms up cooking dinner. We huddle by the fire over coffee, beans and bacon, and Zeke cuts off a salt slab.

"Ah miss the Indian woman fer her cookin'," he says. I do too. Zeke's bannock is hard as brick. We eat it anyway. After pemmican on the trail, anything tastes good. But I offer to cook next, to save our teeth. Once the eating's over, we get back to planning the cabin.

"The wood's too far gone fer usin' again," Zeke says. "We have to start from scratch, and maybe salvage the lean-to for the animal."

Fouter stands like a frozen statue, with frost on his eyelashes and the tips of his ears. Poor beast'll die soon if we don't get him better shelter. He's tied up between our tent and the lean-to wall, but with no roof yet and snow falling about the tent soaking the floor boards beneath us, it's still wretchedly cold. Then as we're finally ready to bed down, we hear a hoarse voice call out "Leclerc! Open up!"

I step outside, Zeke on my heels with his rifle, and find two miners eyeing Fouter. One is tall and sharp featured, the other short and stocky. Both have long beards and need to bathe. The tall man does the talking.

"That's one scrawny mule you got there, friend."

"Looks ain't everything." Zeke's defensive. He's fond of the beast. He's a big man when he stretches up full height. The two look at him in silence, taking his measure.

"I'm Ned Jamieson. This here's Rufus Clark. We work the next claim."

"Kimo," I extend my hand. "This here's Ezekiel and our other partner's up in the Forks. We've taken over Guy's claim." The two exchange surprised looks. They shake my hand but not Zeke's.

"We heard sawing and wondered what was going on. Leclerc kept pretty quiet, all by hisself after his partner left. Don't know as we're surprised he's quit," Jamieson says. But they are. And it's plain they're not happy.

"When did he go?" the tall one asks. "Bastard could've told us. We could've picked up his claim."

"Our partner's seeing the gold commissioner now, doing the transfer, all legal and proper. We're the new owners." I speak conversationally, but emphasize the point.

"No hard feelings. What's done's done. We've got a bottle in our camp. You and your partner come visit when he gets back, see our setup and have a drink." They're not including Zeke. He doesn't blink.

"Thanks. Sorry we can't return your offer; we didn't bring any whiskey with us." I lift our tent flap and they get the message.

"We'll be on our way then."

"They ain't happy we're here," Zeke says when they're gone.

"The claim's ours, and there's nothing they can do about it."

We wake next morning to a white world of silence. I hope Moku found decent shelter for the night. I expect he'll reach the Forks early morning, and head back right away. The cold eats into our bones, in spite of keeping the fire outside going all night, taking turns to throw on wood. We eat and layer on clothes, and pull on gloves for warmth with the fingers cut out so we can hold our tools. Blowing snow creeps in our mouth and eyes, and since we've not shaved every day, ice particles start to form in our beards. Slowly we saw and pile up logs, chipping away the branches as we go. We figure to build our cabin twelve feet by fourteen. We'll need strong posts for the corners, dug into the ground and braced diagonally. We'll cap the peaked roof with shingles split from that cedar log on the riverbank.

We use Guy's leftover planks to square the cabin floor, and start to fit the logs together horizontally for the walls. We build a twelve-foot ladder to reach the roof. We put the ridge pole up, support it on a forked pole at each end, and lay the rafter poles ready for attaching the horizontal ones. We'll put the shingles on them later.

Moku arrives next day after dark. He's hungry, exhausted and so cold his brown Hawaiian skin looks like grey parchment. He draws a bottle of *tanglelegs* from his pack, from the saloon at the Forks, and we fill our tin cups.

"To us!" He waves the paper at me. "I stood in line an hour just to get in the door," he says, "but then it went quickly. I showed Guy's signed statement quitting his claim and made the application to take it over. It was all done in minutes." He tells us over the *tanglelegs* that he reported the man McGregor's death to the gold commissioner's office, and the memory stills our celebration.

I stare at the paper, signed by Thomas Elwyn, gold commissioner for the Cariboo. A dry digging claim covers twenty-five by thirty feet above the river where the water doesn't reach. A bar digging claim covers twenty-five feet wide and extends up to the high water mark and down to low water. Guy's claim is a dry digging with water rights. I can hardly believe we've done it. Staked our own gold claim. Now we can legally work it. The *tanglelegs* warms our bellies and we have no trouble sleeping in spite of the cold.

The cabin's still roofless but we brought a froe, and Zeke's begun to make shingles for it from the cedar rounds. It's slow going. The wood's wet, making it hard to split, and I suspect he's not familiar with cedar, for he's usually quick with all he does. We were lucky to find it. There's not much cedar up here, mostly pine. The cold doesn't help, and Zeke feels it more than we do. The snow is two feet deep now and piling up around us. We shovel it away each night, but by morning it's piled up again, making the tent flaps hard to open. Meantime we're chinking between logs with moss as we go. I've got the wood sawn to frame a door and small window, and wonder if we can bring in a glass pane down from Quesnelle some time.

I want to attach the lean-to to the back of the cabin so I can get Fouter better shelter. It's barely standing now under the snow load with the wind whistling through the cracks. But if I can salvage some of the lumber, I can re-chink it and attach it to the back of the cabin to keep the animal warm. Meantime, I lay cut branches on the rotted floorboards for him, and cover him with bits of sacking off our flour bags, but the wretched beast is still near frozen. I'd hate to lose him.

Next morning we meet Guy's friend Amundsen. The Swede comes gliding in on snowshoes, a giant of a man with a broad chest, ruddy cheeks and a quick smile. He's unshaven with a stringy blond beard, not long, but straggly. His eyes are wide set and a watery blue and his front teeth are set crooked. He introduces himself, and asks after Guy. We tell him he's gone, that we have legally taken over his claim.

"Ah, just as well. In truth, he was here only five minutes before he wanted to leave. Then he got hurt. His partner was a baker. They worked the claim together but it's hard digging, and come start of winter, the baker packed up and left. My claim is two over from yours. Two Spanish brothers, Diego and José Fernandez, work the claim between us. They came up just this summer. Guy was never at peace with them. You'd be wise to keep an eye on your neighbours, both sides. I've another claim down the creek I'm mining right now, but I come up and stick my pan in once in a while here to hold the claim till I'm ready to work it full time. Yes, Guy was a good man, just no miner. He didn't have the know-how or energy to bring water up. I'm sorry I missed him. I've been in Clinton picking up supplies." He winked. "And visiting a lady. What did you say your name was, friend?" he asks Zeke.

"Ezekiel Browne."

"Know anyone like yourself by the name of Jeremiah Carter?"

"No."

"The provincial constable was asking after a black man by that name come up to the goldfields. Six feet tall, big and strong, wanted in California."

"For what?" I ask.

"Murder. Killed a man over the whipping of a black boy in Mississippi. Lawman asked me if I'd seen or heard of such a man, and I said no sir, never heard of no Jeremiah Carter. I reckon if he gets caught, he'll be answering to the Hanging Judge."

He means Begbie, of course. I don't know that the Judge has hung so many. Those he did most likely deserved it.

"Can a man get hung for something he did before he got here?" I ask.

The Swede shakes his head. "I don't know. I'm just passing on the lawman's message."

Zeke pokes the fire with a stick, stirring the ashes. I stare at the flames, as if they should tell me something, but no. My *kupuna* would read messages from the gods in the flames of a fire, but they don't speak to me. Hawaiian gods of heat and sun don't like cold. Only native gods of rivers, trees and animals live here, and maybe the missionaries' Christian god. The flames crackle but tell me nothing. I exchange glances with Moku.

"I've never seen or heard of any Jeremiah Carter," I say.

"Me neither," Moku adds.

Zeke continues to stir the ashes with his stick.

chapter twelve

WITH THREE OF US working hard, the cabin takes shape quickly. Zeke and Moku finish cutting shingles and we throw the roof on as fast as our frozen hands will let us. Jamieson from the next claim comes by now and again to check our progress. It's too cold to work their claim so they've started repairing their sluices and equipment for a quick start-up come spring. He always eyes our camp with the look of a hungry ferret, so we know he's still peeved Guy passed his claim to us, and we're always relieved when he goes.

"We should scout along the river," Zeke says, "when we're done with the cabin. We need to see how other sites are bringing their water in."

"And how the chutes are built," Moku adds, "for that's what we need to start on next. And I'd like to see the hard rock mine that Guy talked about."

It turns out some of our neighbours along the creek are Cornish-men, come from the east, or up from California after thousands left recession at home, the southwest corner of Britain. When they passed through Langley, MacKay told us they were Celtic people, like himself but different, with their own language. They don't speak English but get by with a mix of French, native languages, English and whatever else they can pick up. They know mining, though, having worked in tin and copper mines at home, and men look up to them for their know-how.

November rolls into December and I write to Kami, care of MacKay at the fort. He'll deliver it to the Kwantlen village and read it for her. I write for Moku too, since he can't write. I offer to write for Zeke but he declines. We can send the letters south by Barnard's Express from 150 Mile, or Quesnelle, first time one of us visits for supplies. Moku talked to me before about wanting to learn to read and write. This might be a good time to start. Maybe Zeke will want to as well. We're cooped up here every evening after work, and it would be a better use of time than playing cards.

Zeke's keen even though earlier he didn't want me to send a letter for him. Moku's a bit shy about it, but knows in his heart that he misses opportunities a reading man would have. I start with the English alphabet and progress quickly to easy two- and three-letter words, and they're inordinately pleased when they can write ZEKE and MOKU instead of making an X.

We've met the Indian, Thomas Running Deer, who makes his living transporting goods along the river. He canoes the Quesnelle, then caches his canoe at the junction to our creek, and hauls goods to the miners along the creek using a tumpline, a leather headpiece attached to two ten-foot thongs, which lets him haul up to 300 pounds. He's a Tait Indian, but he married a local Carrier woman. We hired him to fetch another bundle of planks and it takes two weeks, but he arrives with what we want. Our wood he hauls in on a makeshift handcart. I'm pleased when he produces a chit from the sawmill, and charges us only $8 for delivery. He's in no hurry to leave and sniffs the air noisily when Moku starts dinner. It's skunk stew, simmered over the fire with wild onions and dried peas. Skunk is the finest, most delicate meat ever crossed your tongue. Zeke is amazingly good at catching small game, even in the snow.

We invite Thomas to eat with us, and don't need to ask twice. The Indian is short and stocky, like the Kwantlen people, with powerful arm and leg muscles. His face is unlined and seamless, no pock marks, and his brown eyes are clear. We gulp the stew and mop up the gravy with bannock. Afterwards, Thomas draws out a pipe, crams it with tobacco from a leather pouch and sits back.

"My wife is Dakelhne," he tells us. "We live south of the Forks. I have two sons. You come visit. We moved last moon to our *skemel*." A pit house he means, built mostly below ground with sod and grass for walls and roof, with parents, aunts, uncles and cousins all over the place — much like Hawaii when I was a boy. Our *ohana* all lived together in my grandfather's house, too. Now I prefer privacy. Not that I have any at the moment, sharing a room with Zeke and Moku.

"The Q'eyts'i woman spoke of you," the Indian says, drawing the tobacco into his lungs.

"Morning Bird?"

"I see her in Clinton. For many moons she was slave of my people in Yale. She say you buy her?"

"Yes, I did. She's free now." I make her elevated status clear, knowing it will make a difference in how Thomas perceives her. "Is she well? She had a wounded shoulder."

"She spoke nothing of a wound. Say only, the white man she works for has gone south."

"Yes. She looks after his wife and children. Does what's needed." It comes to me that includes preparing and cooking meals, cleaning, making and mending clothes, fetching water and wood, even foraging for food, depending on circumstances, plus being at the family's beck and call night and day. I wonder what they pay her. With room and board off, not much. And I think, it's one thing to choose hardship as we have done, temporarily, but to have no options, with hardship thrust on you for who knows how long — that's another.

"Things are good for her now," he says. "A slave works for the smallest scrap of food. The Q'eyts'i woman gets paid." I suppose a pittance seems like wealth when you're used to deprivation of the worst kind. He changes the subject.

"Your neighbours make trouble." He points to Jamieson's claim. "They stole Leclerc's tools then blamed the Dakelhne people. They tore down fish-drying sheds along the river and said it was others, but our women watched them do it. The miners want us to leave the river, but as long as fish have run, our people have caught and dried them here. They want us out even though this is our land, and the braves grow angry. Our chief came to speak with them but they have no respect."

"Not all miners are like that, Thomas. Decent men will respect your traditions."

"The Q'eyts'i woman say you married Sto:lo," he says, handing me his pipe. I acknowledge the gesture of friendship and draw from it then pass it back. He draws again from the pipe, and hands it to Moku, then to Zeke. I don't want us smoking up the cabin, but now's not the time to say so. I just hope the stream of smoke smarting my eyes finds its way up and out the roof hole I cut.

I ask Thomas to paddle in a stove for our house, but he's not sure one will fit in his canoe.

"When will you be back?" I ask him.

"After fishing," he says. I've lived with the Indians. That can mean this year, next year, sometime, or never. So we'll have to bide our time. It's getting too cold to cook outside so we've made a wide ring in the cabin floor boards for a small fire pit in the bare ground, as in the native longhouses. The smoke goes through the hole in the roof, but the place still reeks. Zeke was worried it would let in the rain and snow, but I rigged a trap for it, so we can close it when the fire's out. We've placed heavy rocks around the pit, and left a good space before the start of the wooden boards, but of course a fire's not safe in a space this small. We need to watch it every second, there being enough burned cabins along the river. Still, our shack's a palace compared to most we've seen.

We're making furniture. Zeke's built frames for making rope beds so we can lift our bedrolls off the cold floor. Moku's weaving the rope across the frames to support our weights. I've hewn a rough table and am working on chairs. We're using pine. It's easier to find up here. The furniture's not fancy, but it'll do. We're weary now, working day in, day out in this damn cold.

We finally get to meet our other neighbours, two brothers from Spain, Diego and José Fernandez. They arrived recently, a few weeks before Guy left. Their shack is poorly built, half of wood with the other half built into the earth of the slope, with a partial corrugated tin roof. But we've never seen its occupants — till now. They come striding across our property with fire in their eyes, waving rifles and raging about us claim jumping. They're small men, and swarthy, with short black beards. Diego, the oldest, has a droopy moustache. They look like twins, although one, José, has half as much hair on his head as the other. They're livid with rage.

"Whoa, there! Just hold on," I say. Claim jumping's a serious charge up here. "This is our claim, and we can prove it. We have the papers from the gold commissioner right here." I haul out the legal papers, and walk with them to pace out each claim peg, numbered as noted on the paper. They appear confused. I don't know why. It's simple enough.

Yet we've heard some miners still don't file claims properly. Maybe it's language difficulties. Maybe it's ignorance. Some miners will just take over a claim from an original owner without registering with the commissioner and it's hard for the authorities to keep up with who's claiming what, and who's walking away leaving claims up for grabs. I point to the paragraph that says we have water rights on the creek. I want them to be clear about this.

"Water rights? What do you mean?" Diego explodes. "A man can take water from a creek for his operation whenever he wants."

"No, he can't. Not unless he's seen the gold commissioner and got permission. If you haven't filed your claim proper, with water rights, that's your problem. We've got water rights for this creek and the papers to prove it. But if it turns out we've more than we need, then I suppose we might sell you some," I say. I know that would be legal.

"Sell us water?" Diego is enraged. Spittle hits his beard. José, the bald one, lifts his rifle.

"Lay down your gun, Fernandez!" Moku barks. He and Zeke have both men in their sights. José lowers his rifle.

"You could be neighbourly." Diego now acts insulted. Then his eyes light up. "We could just add some flumes onto your set-up. It wouldn't take much to divert some water our way."

"No. We're not going to a heap of trouble for your benefit, Fernandez. If you have a problem, take it up with the gold commissioner. You should've thought about water rights when you staked your claim, if you've even done that."

"If we can't draw water from that creek, nobody's getting water from it," Diego swears.

"That's enough!" I say. "Get off our property!" If we trusted them, we might've worked out a deal to provide them with water. Miners can do that, team up to divert water by adding on to flumes to split the flow to different claims. If the Fernandez brothers come back from the commissioner with proof of water rights, we'll do it. Till then, we don't want to make any deal with them. The brothers take off, muttering to each other, hands gesticulating wildly. Moku and Zeke don't lower their rifles till the two of them step off our claim.

"Right friendly neighbourhood," Moku says, "what with Ned and Rufus on one side, and the Fernandez brothers on the other!"

"We just need to stand our ground. Let them know we won't be pushed around, so they'll quit messing with us and leave us alone."

"A rifle's good fer persuadin' at sech times," Zeke drawls.

"That's true. But it just shows how important it is to know your rights." I'm making a point about reading and writing.

"We get it." Moku rolls his eyes, but he's not peeved. He and Zeke are proud of their reading progress and I really don't think I'm pushing them too far too fast.

We decide we won't let our neighbours' peevishness bother us, unless or until we see the paperwork from the gold commissioner. That'll take time. Meantime we've important work to tend to before the weather grows any colder.

Zeke has started to build us a rocker. He's making it from rough lumber and it's about four feet long, eighteen inches high and the same wide. Cleats hold the boards together where the top tray sits. He brought the sheet of metal up in his pack. Two boards, eight feet long form top and bottom ends, the top tapering to the bottom. Pine saplings, two inches in diameter, brace the corners, one a foot and a half, the other three feet long, with two sides squared to fit the corners. The longer sapling tapers to form the handle. The rocking base is made with two pieces of wood nailed together, eighteen inches long, six inches in diameter, bevelled on the ends. On the top, the framed tray sits on cleats. Zeke surveys it critically.

"It's near enough the right shape and size to work," he says. "Ah disremember exac' measurings, but an inch or two here and there don't make much difference. We need to cut strips for riffles then we're done. One top riffle apron will do, but two works better fer breakin' up the gravel, then we'll need a bit of blanket to line the bottom frame."

"We can cut it from that old red rag blanket of Fouter's, and give him one of my spares." Neetlum had advised me to bring extra blankets for trading with the Indians. I don't mind parting with one for the old mule.

We leave the rocker decisions to Zeke, who knows more than we do. All I know is you shovel gravel onto the screen and pour water over it, then rock the box from side to side to wash the fine particles of gravel and gold through the screen into the lower section where the riffles are set. The gold gets caught on the riffles, and the sand and gravel is washed out of the box. We plan to build a sluice box as well, to process more gravel faster. Basically it's a long, wooden trough with riffles along the bottom near the end to catch the gold. You shovel gravel in the box, and pour water through it continuously by means of a flume.

When Zeke's finished the rocker, we head along the creek for a look at the different flumes along the river. We veer off the trail when we spot our neighbour Rufus chopping wood outside his cabin.

"Ned's been gone three days to the Forks for supplies," he tells us. Seems to me Ned's often gone, leaving Rufus with the chores.

"We've started building our equipment, Rufus, and we'd like to see what you've done." If Ned were here, he'd be less than accommodating, but Rufus off leash rises like fish on a line. He can't show us the flumes fast enough.

"Just two side boards and a bottom fastened with cleats," he says. "I made the bottom board wider than the sides, for easy joining. Hardest part was the trestle span crossing the creek. You need strong pole brackets to support the flumes."

Well, they shouldn't be hard to make, we reckon. But it's cold enough to freeze your toes and snow's lying deep on the ground, so we thank Rufus, and head for the Quesnelle River. Just as we figured, we'll need a lot more wood than we've got to complete an entire struc-ture of flumes, brackets, trestle and sluice control box. We'll need to cut more trees, or get the Indian to tow boards in for us from the mill.

"When we git back, Ah kin build the dam we need if you two kin tackle the flumes," Zeke says. Moku and I can do that. We're decent carpenters.

Many cabins are empty along the Quesnelle, men having left for the south, but some are wintering through and when we see smoke, we stop. At times we're welcome, offered precious coffee even, but some miners are withdrawn and suspicious and we move on. Some are repairing gear for next year, working in this miserable cold and snow, but others are purely hibernating. Like bears, hunkering in holes waiting for spring. Some of them have gone strange, paranoid about gear and property, and won't have you stepping on their claims.

"Cabin fever'll get worse before it gets better," Moku says. I think he's right.

Farther along the river we find large group claims. It shakes me, seeing land looking like some savage beast has torn at it with giant teeth and left a huge gaping dark hole and piles of dirt all around. This then, is hard rock mining.

"Diggings get bigger'n bigger as they drill down underground fer nuggets," Zeke says. "Thas where the coarse gold is at, way down deep."

Men have shovelled, opened small holes and pits, then sunk shafts into the ground and run tunnels into the hillsides to carry the gravel and muck in a complex arrangement of sluices. They're using heavy timber to support shafts and tunnels, and a windlass and bucket to raise rock and gravel to the surface. Small carts are piled up outside the tunnels.

"They's railcars," Zeke says, "fer hauling rock up to the surface."

We heard talk in Clinton about this kind of grand mining operation. Men group together to form partnerships to share the costs of extracting deep gold from the quartz rock. Here they're using a Cornish wheel, the first I've seen. They're putting more and more of them up. Seems when water seeped in and flooded shafts, Cornishmen solved the problem using large wooden wheels with shelves. Water from the flumes feeds the wheel. It falls onto the top of the wheel and its shelves, making it turn. The wheel then drives a rocker arm. This in turn pumps water out of the mine shaft. Clever Cornishmen.

But we've seen enough. The blizzard that's blowing stings our eyes and whirling snow slaps at our faces so we head back to the cabin. We wrap our wool scarves so just our eyes are showing, but the frost creeps in anyway, crisping our beards and eyebrows. I think if we touch them, they'll fall off. Trekking is sheer misery in this hellish cold.

"You smell somethin'?" Zeke moves his scarf from his nose to sniff the air as we return to Beaver Creek from the river.

"Smoke," Moku says. "Something's burning."

We can't see through the blizzard, and we're almost home, nearing Ned Jamieson's place, when we spot the plume of grey smoke funnelling skyward.

"A cook fire?"

"Somebody's clearing, burning stumps."

"In this weather?"

Strange combination, smoke and snow, heat and cold, I think, as we toil through the drifts along the track, towards home, if you can call our shack home. We pass Jamieson's claim, but neither he nor Rufus are anywhere to be seen.

"Smoke's gittin' worse," Zeke says. "Kin you hear somethin'?"

At first nothing, but then I do. A mule braying frantically.

"Fouter!" I break into a run.

Moku shouts. "It's us!"

Zeke streaks past us both, reaches the shack first. Blackened stumps are all that's left of our west wall, and part of the roof is about to cave in. Fire is licking across the roof shakes, eating into the north wall. Behind it, the lean-to is in flames and Fouter is kicking his hind legs in panic. He rolls his head and bites insanely at me when I fight to loosen his tethers. I can smell the hair singeing on his back as he heaves into the air with his hind legs, braying then making a strange strangled sound like a human baby. I feel sick. He trots away limping, bucking feebly before toppling to the ground in a shaking heap.

Zeke and Moku are bucketing water from the creek in tin pails, running, stooped over, Moku bow-legged from the weight, heaving it on the fire. I join them as snow falls on the heaps of blackened ashes, meeting the heat then bursting into tiny silent flumes of steam.

A handful of men tumble through the snow from along the creek, ones working their claims and others we've never seen, come out of their wintering places. Amundsen arrives and helps form a water line from the creek to the shack. It seems fire's common among the shack dwellers and they're ready to lend a hand as credit for the day their own may burn. No sign of our neighbours, Ned Jamieson or Rufus, though.

"Our gear!" I holler at Moku, and quit the water line. We wrap our-selves in wet blankets. Years before, Fort Langley had burnt to the ground, and we all lost everything in the fire but for a few furs and a handful of food items, and struggled for survival afterwards. Memories of that hardship spur us on.

We charge into the shack. The door's smoking, but the flames haven't yet eaten into it. I pick up a bundle of gear and toss it from the shack. Zeke's there now, waving his arms at us. Moku sends a bundle soaring. It lands at Zeke's feet. He lifts it and tosses it to safety. I heave a sack of food supplies at him. Moku snatches at clothes and tools and throws them at Zeke and I lift and heave whatever I can pick up. We pitch bundle after bundle till the smoke gets to us and the wet blankets have stopped steaming. Hot and now dried out, they offer no protection. Our eyes sting and Moku begins coughing so hard I yell "Out!" and shove him towards clean air, just as water rains down on us from outside. Thank God. The men are gaining on the flames and we are doused as we stagger outside.

Some men on the water line had been hostile when we called on them earlier. Now they cheer for us as the flames flare and die, flare and die again, and again, till finally only smoldering ashes remain. Moku wags his thumb and little finger at me and we exchange sooty grins.

We thank the men for coming. One fetches a whiskey flask from his back pocket, passes it around. Every last man appreciates the swig, feeling the raw cold again now the flames have been beaten back. Fire over, all talk turns to gold, to Richfield and Stout's Gulch in Barkerville, and Camerontown, and Marysville and the big strikes being made. Horsefly and Keithley creeks are spent, and Antler Creek staked out, but William's Creek is paying out big, pounds of gold a day to Cunningham and Company, three thousand dollars a day, they say. Every man believes there's more gold to be found, that he'll be the one to find it.

Thank God we're close to the water. Thank God for the snow falling. Thank God we returned home when we did. It's odd though, watching a fire die through flakes of snow the size of walnuts.

"Could be worse," Moku says. "But the west wall's gone, and the north wall's down to black stumps."

"We lost half the roof as well," Zeke says. "This ain't jes bad luck. Ah put water on that fire afore we left, not once but twice."

"You saying this was set deliberate, Zeke?"

"There was nuthin' there to start no fire. Nuthin'. Ah doused every single ash in that pit, scraped it through an' doused it again."

"Scout around. I'll join you after I see to Fouter."

I draw a bucket of creek water and wipe the shaking animal down with cold wet cloths. I don't know what to do for him. I try to dab his back where flying bits of burned wood touched down and scorched his hair, but he recoils from the salve I find in my pack and brays when I touch him, so I stay with the cool water and cover him with a blanket, picking the cleanest one I can find. It smells of smoke — everything does — and it makes him skittery, but he needs to be covered, what with the shock and the damn cold.

I assess the damage. Parts of the roof fell into the cabin and now shakes are heaped in a black pile on the floor. I root around the smoldering pile. Beneath the burned top, some remain intact, others are partially burned. I throw a pail of water at the pile. With luck, we can salvage some. The poles of the two side walls are reduced to black stumps. They'll need replacing. Moku's carefully built beds and Zeke's table and chairs are ruined. Weeks of work, for nothing. We kept some gear outside in the lean-to with Fouter. The tools are intact, but we've lost some food and clothing bundles. Still, we're lucky we salvaged what we did.

Moku hollers from our claim line. "There's something here you should look at."

I plod towards him through the scuffed snow. He points at three sets of recent prints separate from the others, leading from Jamieson's claim to ours. "What do you think?"

"One large pair, and two smaller sets." I squat and study the imprints in the snow. The large set shows a distinct criss-cross pattern, like my own. They've come directly from our neighbour's claim. We return to the cabin, and review the day's events.

"Who'd set fire to our shack?" Moku asks, "and why?"

"It can't be the Indians," Zeke says. "We done nothing to rile 'em. Their fishing sheds were wrecked afore we got here."

"Those prints are from boots, not mukluks. And they all come from

Jamieson's claim. Neither Ned nor Rufus came to help, yet they had to smell the smoke. My guess is Ned and the Fernandez brothers made those prints," Moku says.

We trek through the snow to Ned and Rufus's cabin and rap sharply on the door. Rufus answers after our second pounding.

"Where's Ned?"

"Downriver, visiting friends." He's edgy. Won't look us in the eye.

"Our cabin burned, Rufus. You must've smelled the smoke?"

"I figured you were clearing." He stares at the space behind my ear.

"Leclerc cleared the claim long before we came. You know that. Somebody set fire to our cabin deliberate, and made prints in the snow that lead right here."

"I know nothin' about your fire," Rufus says defiantly. The snow's coming down hard, piling in the open doorway, blowing against his body and laying a white film on his hair. He shakes his head and it showers over his shoulders. He draws the door towards him, and takes hold of the bolt. "A bad night's setting in. I got nothing more to say. Be on your way."

Moku sticks his foot out to prevent the door from closing and jabs Rufus hard on the shoulder. Moku's uptight. Superstition has a toe-hold on him still. Me, too. It's the Hawaiian in us. In the old days we believed the goddess Pelé created all fire. The missionaries taught otherwise, of course, and we left off being followers of the old ways but when fire happens, those early fears of Pelé's anger rise to haunt you, hovering outside logic.

Moku kicks the door with his foot, but Rufus stops it from opening further with his shoulder. "If you want a man to believe you, Rufus, look him in the eye. This isn't over. Your friends might have started something, but we'll finish it. Hear me?" Moku spits in the snow as Rufus slams the door and slides the bolt into place.

Back at the shack, Zeke has shovelled the burned shakes off the floor, and sorted them in piles to reuse or throw away. And so we begin again. Each day dawns like the day of a battle. We fight to rebuild, to make any small progress in this dreadful Cariboo cold — cold so bitter it numbs your brain as well as your body parts. I can hardly move my fingers, and my feet are layered in socks in my boots but they've no feeling.

Thomas hauls in wood after news of the fire spreads along the creek. He won't be able to canoe much longer, the way the river's icing over. We work till we drop every day. We rebuild the cabin board by board but we'll need more nails and more wood for the flumes. It's been sleeting hail for days, and drying our clothes stinks up the cabin. The wet woollens and wet leathers make my nose twitch and I spend my nights sneezing.

I haven't slept much since the fire. Those boot prints in the snow have been gnawing at me. Most miners around here are smaller than Moku, Zeke and I. The small prints could belong to anyone. To the Fernandez brothers, if Moku's right, for they're still angry with us over the water rights. The large prints have me puzzled though. They're from studded boots like mine, from the Hudson's Bay store. Few miners wear boots that size. Ned's could be that big, but he's not stayed around for us to check. Even if his boots are that big, it's hardly proof enough he set our fire, though he surely does resent us taking over Guy's claim from right under his nose.

Diego and José have been visiting Rufus in the evenings in his shack. We watch them stumble their way home through knee-deep snow after a night of drinking, firing off their pistols for no good reason, their whiskey-fuelled shouts echoing through the cold night air. When Diego fires his rifle into the night air above our cabin once too often, I decide enough's enough and confront him.

"Next time you pull that trigger near our cabin, Fernandez, I'll take it you're firing at us."

"Take it however you want," he replies.

"I'm warning you. Shoot our way one more time, bullets are coming back at you." That's the end of his shooting at us. With some people, you have to push back.

We've been so jumpy since the fire, we're suspicious of every tiny sound, leaping like shot rabbits at the snap of a tree branch, at the scurrying of mice feet in the cabin, at the scrabbling of tiny mammals foraging through snow and dead leaves beside our door, even at the hoot of an owl. Rose called that the death bird. I could never understand why. It's a pretty sound, soft as a Hawaiian dove's cry. Yet now, hearing it makes me jump like a scalded cat. The three of us are wound up tight as springs. This damn cold has crept so deep into our bones and brain, none of us can think straight.

chapter thirteen

THE COLD CLAWS AT our fingers, toes, noses. It cramps the chest till you can hardly breathe. Not for the first time, I think hell is no place of fire, but of ice and cold. Zeke's miserable, and talks to himself in an effort to stay sane.

Rose still comes to me at night in dreams. She straps Kami on her back. Khatie ties on Keiki, then they lift their baskets and set out to pick berries.

"Rose!" I call but she doesn't hear and they disappear into the trees laughing, babies jiggling on their backs, and I call and call till my voice grows hoarse rising through the trees, scattering ravens, black dots, screeching into the air.

Moku shakes me awake and reality sets in. The Cariboo cold wraps round me like a vise again. How much more of this we can take? Fouter's come back strong, though, pawing his way through the snow each morning to eat the grass below, and his tethered walkabouts have cleared much of what's falling around the shack. We've repaired the walls and the roof shingles and rebuilt the furniture. But we need more wood to build flumes, and Thomas hasn't been here since his visit after the fire. We also need to replace food supplies, so one of us has to go to the Forks. It must be me as Moku went last time, and besides, he's sick, coughing and sneezing, and the cold has sent Zeke into himself, muttering and humming strange tunes.

I don't know what to expect when I lace on my snowshoes and head out with Fouter. We trek the creek to the Quesnelle River then head east. Ice is forming on the river in great white patches now. Dark purple clouds have rolled in from the north. Looks like more snow's coming. The air roils with energy and the wind combing through the trees sounds like a swarm of bees. The world's a white blanket and I'm stiff with the cold and everything's numb. Including my trigger finger. I work my fingers to and fro inside my mitts till I feel the stiffness ease.

There's a muddle of prints on the trail's fresh snow. One set stands out more than the others — large, like my own studded Hudson's Bay boots. I squat beside the tracks, willing them to tell me something. And the thought occurs to me that the Company chose big men when they recruited Hawaiians. Few are as big as me. Ahuhu's one of them. "We're not done yet," he'd said, when I sent him packing in Langley.

My mind races with possibilities. Is he stalking us? Could Ahuhu have set our fire? The prints would fit. Was he the shooter in Yale, aiming for me and hitting Morning Bird by mistake? If so, he's lost his touch. He used to be a crack shot, but he's been sick for so long. Fort runaways can't always find mercury treatment for venereal disease after deserting. But sick or well, he's a troublemaker. And dangerous. Always was. If these are his tracks, he'll have to show himself soon. He'd like nothing better than to put a bullet in me, I know. This damn cold must be freezing my brain. I can't think straight.

Each breath feels like an icicle piercing my lungs. I ignore the pain. I need to stay strong, to blot out this casket cold. I play tricks in my mind and pretend I've crossed the sea, that I'm drifting on warm waves back to the Islands. In my imagination, the dark overhead light changes to warm gold then to a bright orange ball hovering over a blue horizon and I arrive in "the gathering place," beautiful Oahu. Sunlight shimmers on the surface of the water and heat waves undulate along the shore. Palm fronds tremble with the soft touch of the trade wind's breeze as men and women lie on the sand and children laugh in the shallows. An ache of warmth seeps into my veins, and melts the cold clutching my heart.

A sudden sharp rifle crack splits the air and I drop to the ground, ripped back into the cold Cariboo, fumbling for my rifle. A burst of pain sears my left shoulder and I feel a hot poker knifing into my flesh. Blood seeps up through the layers of woollens beneath my coat and I think foolishly, at least it's warm. The smear of red spreads, fans out on the fabric of my coat. How could I have been so damned stupid?

Another shot, an unearthly scream and Fouter's back arches. He drops on his two front knees, screeching. The mule turns his head and looks at me, brown eyes wide with fear and pain, then his hindquarters judder and heave and he topples sideways, braying and gasping for breath. I spot a glint of metal through the trees. The bastard's up there. I hunker behind the whimpering mule. His body is jerking in spasms. A stream of blood fans out from the bullet hole just above his stifle, where his left hind leg joins his gut. I thought he was gut shot but it looks like it might have lodged in the muscle, so he may have a chance. I feel sick for him and rub my hand along his side, smoothing his patchy coat, whispering comfort lies in his ear, "Whoa, Fouter, old boy. Be still. You'll be all right." I hate the thought that I might have to put the mule out of his misery.

I scan the trees for signs of a rifle. Whoever it is, he's not moving. He wants to make sure he got me. But I'm going after him. It's my left

shoulder that's shot. I've still got a good right arm. I roll behind Fouter's rump into a clump of bushes. My shoulder hurts like hell. Losing
Fouter would hurt more. I haul off my snowshoes and creep bush to
bush, half crawling, half hauling myself up the low snow-covered hillside. He's still there, not far now. I move silently, trying not to breathe
hard, for he might see me coming from the steam my breath makes.
Then suddenly I'm there.

I lean back against a thick pine, bracing myself in the deep snow. I
feel weak but I have him in my sights, not thirty feet away. My rifle is
ice cold. The smooth brass plate with the dragon serpent, symbol of
the Hudson's Bay rifle, feels slick as a dead fish in my hands. I pray it
doesn't jam. My trigger finger feels numb, lifeless, and it hits me that
this Cariboo cold could be the death of me if the damn rifle seizes up.

"Here!" I bark. He swings his rifle in a wild arc towards me and
fires. Too fast. The bullet hits the trunk with a thwack inches above
my head, but then I pull the cold trigger. I hear the shot but he stays
upright staring at me, dark eyes bulging. I think I've missed, and raise
the rifle to shoot again, but my shoulder is pained from the recoil of
the rifle and I suddenly feel weak. My legs buckle and I slide slowly
down the tree trunk then watch as he pitches forward headfirst into
the snow.

"Damn, I got him, Fouter." My breath steams the air. It's cold. So
cold, I feel like sleeping but I know I mustn't. But I can rest awhile.
I'll have to report his death to the authorities in Quesnelle Forks.
He'll need to be buried. I try to stand up, using the rifle as a cane but
my shoulder burns and my legs won't co-operate so I slump down on
the snow again, back against the pine tree. I take a deep breath and
try again, but freeze. There's a noise coming up the trail, a new sound,
and the crackle of branches. I snatch up my rifle again. What traveller
fights through untrod snow in the forest rather than use a packed
trail? I hold my breath then I see him. It. A brown bear, lumbering my

way and I can't fathom why a damn bear is roaming around this time of year instead of hibernating. I lift my rifle unsteadily, fingers feeling fat and lifeless as cold sausage. I fumble as the bear approaches.

"Kanui!" The beast has a voice. Two black eyes peer at me. I lower my rifle.

"For God's sake, Thomas! I could've killed you." White teeth flash through a head hood trimmed with fox fur. His entire body is covered with a man-size bear pelt.

"What're you doing here?"

"My *skemel* up there," he points. "Hear shots, come quick. You bleed bad?"

"I took a bullet in the shoulder. I just killed a man."

"*Whaah!*"

"Help me up, Thomas. I want to see his face." I haul myself to my feet, lean on him and we stumble towards the body that snowflakes are already beginning to cover. Thomas turns him over and I draw a deep breath and shock courses through me. I'm looking into the dead staring eyes of Diego Fernandez. A small hole mid-chest is seeping blood. It's bubbling up through a hole in his coat, and the stain's spreading across the fingers he's splayed against the hole. I hit his heart. A quick death. His dark face stares up at me, little eyes bulging with shock, mouth open showing uneven chipped teeth. He didn't have buck teeth, but they did stick out some and he's missing one. Now blood from his mouth is trickling down his chin and clumping in his beard. It occurs to me the last time you look at a man is much like the first time, you remember everything you see. I feel sadness at the sight of the little man spread-eagled before me, at his face, at the little veins riddling his hooked nose, at his vacant eyes, like tiny black peas, staring up at the sky, at his black hair, separated at the crown and pushed behind his ears. I have trouble breathing.

The cold must have addled my brains. The large prints had me fooled. I thought they'd be Ahuhu's, but they must belong to some other man, some innocent miner trekking north, going about his business and having nothing whatsoever to do with me.

"Whaah! Much *pilpil*," says Thomas.

"Yes. Lots of blood. I should bury him."

"Ground too hard. We can tree him. You come. My winter house not far."

"He shot my mule. I need to get my packs off him first." Fouter's breathing hard when we get there. Thomas lifts one bundle off the mule and I the other, then he helps me re-fasten my snowshoes. Fouter's confused by the smell of Thomas in the bear skin, and brays feebly. Thomas feels around the bullet hole.

"*Lemule* hurt. We can fix, maybe." He lays a hand on my arm. "*Chaco*," he says, telling me to come. I throw a blanket over Fouter and follow Thomas along the riverbank till finally he points ahead. I don't see his *skemel* at first, it blends so well with the landscape, built in a circle of earth and wood and dug halfway into the ground. Thomas removes my gear and tosses it down inside the house, then I climb with him down a rough wooden ladder. Each rung is a challenge, as my left arm is dangling uselessly, but my feet finally touch the dirt floor. It's warm but smoke from the indoor fire nearly chokes me. When my eyes adjust to the smoky haze, I count eight men and women, eleven children and two babies, all wearing furs of one kind or another.

"Family," Thomas says, waving at the group of relatives, brothers, cousins, wives and an old grandmother. They greet me with silent curiosity. Bear skins cover the floor and furs stack in piles on beds, low shelving built around the walls.

"My wife," he says, as a young woman with a pretty smile steps forward. She's covered in furs so I can't tell if she's large or small. The children stare at me wide-eyed, a little fearful. One little girl reminds me of Kami.

"The man was tracking you," Thomas says. "No see?" I shake my head. "My people have better eyes and ears," he says with conviction.

The elders have lit pipes and squat cross-legged, smoking in a circle. They talk among themselves, blowing smoke into air thick as cooked porridge. Thomas asks his wife for water to clean my wound. I take off my coat and shirts. Two older women chattering like jays mix up some kind of grey paste. They giggle. I think they joke at my expense, but they clean me up and plaster paste over the wound and cover it with what looks like mustard and cobwebs.

"You find doctor at the Forks," Thomas says. "Take out many bullets."

Thomas' wife offers me a wooden bowl with some kind of stew, hot and meaty with onions, that I gobble up hungrily. Thomas pulls a mat near the fire and throws a bear skin on it.

"Sleep now."

I hadn't planned on staying, but my knees won't hold me up. I stretch out under the bear pelt, tired to the bone. It's not every day you kill a man. Or be so wrong. I toss and turn till late morning, and wake with a throbbing shoulder. I need to get this bullet out before the wound turns septic, though the cobweb paste the Carrier women spread over it has eased the pain. The pit house is empty but for one old woman, who points at the fire. A solid slab of grey porridge dotted with dried berries sits in the pot. She nods encouragement. I'm hungry and eat it all before taking my leave for the Forks.

I struggle up the ladder and outside find men fussing around a travois, and damned if Fouter isn't lying on it under a heap of blankets and pelts. He's still alive, huffing vapor, a layer of snow coating his back like the stripe on a skunk. They've no horses or mules, so they must've used their dogs to haul him here. I squat beside Fouter and stroke his old back. I blow softly up his nose. I've seen Zeke do this. I don't know why, or what it does, but it always seems to reassure him.

"Not dead yet," Thomas says. "We wait."

I thank him and strap on my snowshoes. Zeke bought them used from a miner at 150 Mile, and patiently mended them. I wouldn't want to slog through the heavy snow that's fallen overnight without them. Thomas hands me a bear pelt.

"Keep you dry." I wrap it round my shoulders and tie it with strips of sewn-on sinew. "Hee! Men on the trail will think bear coming," Thomas laughs as I head out into the cold to the Forks.

And when at last I cross the new bridge into the Forks, I'm exhausted, frozen except for my shoulder. It's hot and beating like a drum, and I feel queasy. The Forks is another town sprung up to meet the needs of miners, surrounded by mountains, built on the flat between the rivers, Quesnelle and Cariboo. No place to set a town, I'm thinking, but shacks and miners' tents line the road in, and snow's been cleared in parts and there's planks here and there for walking on, so I sit and haul off my snowshoes. Somebody's chained a raccoon to the side of a saloon. Seems cruel in this cold, but maybe it's a pet that gets taken in nights. The town's alive with miners — hundreds, maybe thousands. They're savvy, geared up for the cold, mostly unshaven, wearing blanket coats, boiled and greased wool scarves and hats, sheepskin mitts. Some go Indian style with fur pelts slung over shoulders. There are stores, hotels, rooming houses, eating places, laundries, all with water barrels on the roofs, in case of fire and there's Chinamen everywhere. I find the town police constable in the barbershop and tell him of Diego Fernandez, naming Thomas as witness, and that's the end of it. But when I'm through, every ounce of energy leaves me and I can't stand without weaving.

"I got a bullet in me," I tell the barber. "Where can I find a doctor?"

"Doc's gone up to Barkerville. Sorry, friend, I can pull teeth, but can't take out a bullet. You got gold enough to pay for doctoring?"

"How much?"

"Got anything against Chinamen? They got their own medicine

and they'll do it cheap, if you know who to ask."

"Who would that be?"

"Me," he says, dipping his barber shears into a jar of liquid. "Hong Lee!" From the rear of the shack, sandals scuffle across a floor and a young Chinaman appears.

"Customer here's got hisself shot up. Can you look after him?"

"You come please, come please." The boy bobs and curtsies and opens the door. I follow. He looks sixteen, but you can't tell with Chinamen. He's likely older. A long queue falls down his back. He wears a Chinese top and black pants, but covers himself in a western overcoat for going outside, and hauls on stout leather boots. We turn behind the barbershop into a narrow lane and turn and turn again, and he stops outside a small store window full of powders and jars and tiny green vials.

Inside, the boy speaks with an elderly Chinaman who stares at me unblinking through pea-sized eyes. His face is spotted with dark moles above a drooping moustache, and a long white thin beard reaches to his chest. His bald head's speckled like a mottled egg. Hong Lee indicates a small cot against the wall. I remove my gear and sit down. On the table beside the cot is a basketful of withered poppies. For making laudanum, I expect. The old man soaks some cotton with liquid from a green bottle and holds it to my mouth and the last thing I hear is Hong Lee's "You sleep, please," in my ear.

When I wake on the cot, the room is dark and my shoulder's wrapped in bandages. Clean ones. There's no sign of the old Chinaman.

"You wake now. Want tea?" I nod, take the tiny pink and green floral cup from Hong Lee, and the hot tea goes down in two gulps. It tastes oddly of flowers. He pours me another. "Bullet out," he says. "Forty dollah."

Cheap. A shovel costs sixteen dollars up here. The shoulder aches and throbs, but not as bad as before. I hand him the money.

"You want?" He rolls the bullet back and forth in his small calloused palm then hands it to me.

"No." I want nothing to remind me of the man I killed. A difference over water rights should never have triggered this violence. Men like Diego are prideful, and brook no opposition. They turn violent whenever things don't go their way. Moku guessed right. Diego must have set the fire — no doubt with Ned's help, in retaliation for us "stealing" his claim. I drop the bullet in a saucer of pipe ash on the table by my cot.

"Can I go?" I ask Hong Lee. He nods, fetches my shirts and coat and fur pelt, my snowshoes and gear and gives me a tiny packet of white powder wrapped in a small square of paper screwed up at the end.

"For sleep."

I leave as he bows and bobs. I bow back, feeling foolish but think it's the thing to do. Miners talk of Chinamen and their secret societies. I know nothing of these things. Only that they work hard, have their own ways and don't act foolish. I find a mill and hardware store and order planks to be delivered by Thomas. I'll carry the nails.

"You're lucky. This is the last bag in the store," the storekeeper says. "Three dollars a pound. Next shipment the price is going up." I think he's making more money than any miner.

In the general store I buy fifty pounds of flour, thirty pounds of tea, a five-pound bag of salt, thirty pounds of beans and eighteen pounds of bacon, and have to pay $130. There's just no getting round the high price of food up here. With Fouter shot, and no money for a new mule, I'll carry what I can in my pack. The rest Thomas can deliver when he gets round to it.

I head for the saloon. Men are hollering, fighting in a back corner, throwing punches. Shots go off but they don't raise an eyebrow in the place. The bartender talks calmly of three men killed here last summer, found shot in the head in Murderer's Gulch, near the bridge. A fight boils up again and I leave when both men sport black eyes and things are getting serious. I find a room and take to bed early. The Chinaman's twist of powder is in my pocket but I'm so tired I don't need it.

Next day I prepare to head back to the claim. The raccoon that was chained at the saloon has gone . . . only a piece of carcass lying on the ground remains, covered with dirty snow in a pool of blood, and a sled dog licking at it. I wish now I'd loosened him off that chain when I first set eyes on him. I walk against the blowing wind, boots falling deeper and deeper into the snow till I lace on my snowshoes where Quesnelle's road gives way to the trail.

There's no getting used to this cold. It sucks the life out of you, and the wind tears through you like a blade cuts paper. The river corkscrews its way west through the chunks of ice forming on it. I wonder when Thomas will be able to deliver our supplies. I locate his pit house by nightfall, and find Fouter outside, tethered in a makeshift shelter of pelts. He's covered with furs and, to my surprise, is upright. He snorts and snuffles till I dump the bear skin off my shoulder and then he stands still, sniffing and tossing his head about, staring at me with his big mule eyes. Tufts of his winter hair are coming out. He looks like a chair losing its stuffing.

"Hey, old thing. You're doing fine." I put my arm around his neck, run my hands down his left hind leg, feel the muscle and find the wound. A paste now covers the hole; leaves of some kind cover the paste. He brays when I touch it.

"*Hai*, Kanaka! You back." Thomas appears with two other natives through the trees. Natives always seem to appear out of nowhere.

"It's good to see the mule on his feet."

"The bullet found his muscle. We dig out. He well soon."

"Can he travel?"

"Wait some days. And you?"

"My shoulder's healing. A Chinaman at the Forks dug out the bullet." This amuses Thomas and he passes the information to the two other men, who laugh out loud with him. We climb down the ladder into the smoky pit house, and I'm glad to be out of the raw cold and among friends. I tell Thomas what I bought at the Forks, and he agrees to fetch the supplies for us when he can.

"Now is too soon for your *lemule*. Can't haul on bad leg."

"I can pick him up in a week or so. But I have to get back as soon as I can. We're short on camp supplies."

We smoke and he tells me they treed the Spaniard. His body lies in a wooden crib stuck up on poles twenty feet from the ground, leaning against a large pine. They hung his possessions, his overcoat and his gun on the platform with him. Indians are respectful of the dead, even if respect is undeserved. I thank Thomas for that. Their furs keep me warm and soon sleep comes, though the house smells of smoke and food and sweat, and men are snoring like drumbeats through the night. I leave after breakfast after brushing down Fouter. I hate to leave him, but he'll heal faster if I don't push him too soon.

It's slow going back to the claim, now I'm carrying this heavy pack of supplies from the Forks, with only one good shoulder. Another storm's blowing in, shucking down hail the size of peas. My chin and ears and the tip of my nose are blue, and the condensation of my breath evaporates slowly like smoke in the cold air. The ground's frozen and the snowshoes are slicking along so fast I can hardly balance on them, so I take them off, fingers fumbling, and tie them behind my shoulders beneath the pack. Along the trail I pass a dying coyote smeared in blood, and a dead moose that some hungry miner will no doubt skin and eat before I can get back to claim him.

I arrive back at the claim, where Moku and Zeke greet me as if I've been gone a month.

"Aloha!" Moku throws his arms about me. Zeke squirms. Our Hawaiian ways embarrass him. I've tried to explain *aloha* to him, how it's both a greeting and farewell, how it signifies affection, sympathy, kindness, love. How it's the essence of Hawaiian life, of hospitality, friendship, giving, sharing. Zeke shakes my hand, pumping my arm up and down so hard, it hurts.

"Mind the shoulder! I had a bullet in it for two days. Diego Fernandez shot me."

"*Auwé*! Fernandez?" Moku says.

"On the trail north. But I got him. He's dead." Zeke makes a growling noise in his throat. "Thomas took me to his *skemel* and the women cleaned my wound. He'll fetch the rest of our supplies when he can." I change to dry clothes, and we talk long into the night before turning in.

I dream tonight of Rose. Again, she's berry-picking with Khatie and the children. I watch as plump ripe salmonberries roll from the bushes into her palm, but as she turns, it's not Rose after all, but Morning Bird, smiling, and carrying a wicker basket. I wake with a start. Then I reach for the Chinaman's white powder, and sleep like the dead.

We spend our days repairing the last of the fire damage to the cabin. The furniture's mostly finished. A plank wood table and three sanded chairs. We've even a tray for forks and spoons, and some rough door-less shelving on one wall, stacked with enamel plates and cups. Thomas snowshoes in two weeks later with Fouter hauling a sled loaded with planks.

"*Lemule* better," he says. "Get mean soon."

"He ain't never mean," Zeke says. He's as fond of the beast as I am. "He jes don't like toting a heavy load o' lumber fer miles." Fouter's wound has healed but he still favours his leg. I take off his reins, walk him to his shelter and rub him down before I blanket him. He rubs his forehead up and down on my chest again and again, and I fancy he's glad to see me too.

"Thanks for your help, Thomas. Your family, too. I appreciate it."
He'll stay overnight, of course. Natives have little sense of urgency.
What we call wasting time, they call time well spent. Hawaiians never
felt pressure about time either. I learned it after coming here. Moku
serves up peas and bacon and biscuits and we talk late into the night.

"Your Q'eyts'i woman was in Clinton last full moon," Thomas says.
"The children's mother has died."

"She had a cough. I expect it was consumption."

"Morning Bird will stay with children till the father comes back
from Oregon with horses. Good if they're horses, bad if like the beasts
on Clinton trail."

"What beasts?" Moku asks.

"Big, brown, like horse with two bumps on the back. Better to carry
heavy loads, men say, but I saw one eat a shoe and a shirt and pants,
and start on a saddle. What they pull into their mouths, they eat. And
spit!" Thomas spits himself. "Our spirits do not want them here. This
is not their place."

"You must've been into the *tanglelegs* in Clinton, Thomas," Moku
says, but I recall hearing about them in the saloon when I was at the
Forks.

"It's true, Moku. They're called camels. Someone from Lillooet
brought twenty-three of them up from California to freight goods to
Alexandria. Twelve of them are wintering over at the Forks. I didn't
see them myself, but it was the talk of the saloon. Their feet are too
soft though, so they're making canvas boots for them."

"You're making this up," Moku retorts.

"Ask the Barnard's Express men. They hate them. Their horses bolt
with fright when they see them coming."

We ponder the coming of the camels, and the strange times we live
in, then light our pipes and fall into silence. Thomas leaves next
morning, a black fur ball sliding on snowshoes, under a milky sky dur-

ing a lull in the blizzard caroming up the river. He wears a small rectangle of bone over his eyes with slits to see through. I think I'll make me a pair. The cold air has frozen the wet snow, encasing Fouter in a shell of ice in spite of the blankets and pelts he has to lie on. I tack extra planks around his shelter, overlapping the joints that let in the wind and snow.

Now we have to start building flumes. We've frost on our lashes, and chilblains on our feet. We've chapped lips and fingers paralyzed with cold, and snow and pea hail keep shucking down. But we have to be ready come spring. We've too much to lose if we're not.

chapter fourteen

WEATHER'S CHANGING. NOT MUCH, but we can feel it, though it's still snowing and the cold hasn't eased up yet. I went to speak with José. At first he was hostile, and I thought there might be trouble, but after some heated discussion he acknowledged Diego's temper and accepted I had the right to defend myself. Moku has started building the flumes. They're simple to put together and he's got a pile stacked up already. Each needs three boards, two sides and a bottom, supported across the top with cleats. Since the creek's begun to thaw now, Zeke and I walk up the creek to find the height we need for building our dam. Zeke picks a spot at a bend where a boulder at the edge of the creek blocks the water, constricting the flow between the banks.

"We kin fell these pine trees fo' a start," he says. There's one on each side of the creek. "And we'll run the flume down the right bank, and cross it over when we git farther down."

We haul the pines across the creek till they join up, then pile earth and rocks behind them. I wonder how we'd have figured all this out without Zeke. There's no way to avoid getting soaked. The water's killing cold and we're miserable. We don't talk, just pile on the rocks till eventually a pool forms behind it.

"It leaks," Zeke says when we think we're finished. "Needs more rock."

We plug the dam over and over till finally it holds, and Zeke concedes, "That should do it."

We line up Moku's flumes along the creek to see how many we need. We make pole brackets to hold them up, and build a trestle to support them across the creek. Zeke puts together another flume with a top on it, and fits it in place to take the water from under the dam. We jam it with big rocks to hold it in place then we join all the flumes together.

We celebrate the night we finish them, with the last of the *tanglelegs* Moku brought from the Forks. We're weary and sick of being cooped up in this damn shack, yet we've done it . . . finished the flumes and we're ready to dig as soon as the ground warms up some more. Now March is over, miners are slowly surfacing, creeping around claims like turtles inside their shells, unshaven, unwashed, some gone strange and as like to shoot you if you call to them. No one's given us trouble though, not even Ned Jamieson and Rufus, since word spread along the river about Fernandez. Thomas had something to do with that, I suspect. We keep to ourselves, keep busy and keep clean. Zeke brought scissors. Seems another thing he did in San Francisco was barbering. He cuts our hair and reminds us when we go too long between shaves. Moku sneezes so hard during one cut, Zeke accidentally clips a chunk of hair off the top of his head and it ends up looking like the short stalks in a cut hayfield.

The sky's been teasing us days on end with watery sunshine but it's finally broken through and melt-water from the mountains comes coursing over the frozen ground. The body of a dead caribou pokes up from the melting snow banks by the trail. The site's flooded and another storm breaks. Rain falls down like rods, then a raging torrent of hail descends and turns into coarse wet snow. Northern natives have names for different kinds of snow. I wonder what they'd call this. Each day miners check the river level, every miner thinking of the gold being churned up and hauled along in the rushing water.

Thomas won't canoe the river when it's this wild. He brings supplies in on foot or by sled when he pleases, but we never know when to expect him or how long he'll stay. When he does appear, someone's with him, and as they draw near, he calls out "*How Oihes*! The *kloochman* is with me," and beneath the fur capes, we find ourselves staring into the eyes of the Indian woman.

"Morning Bird! What are you doing here? Did Hesse come back already?"

"No."

"Then where are the children?"

"The *Wakeskokuin* family took them." She means the English family.

"The Hawthorns? Why?"

"It is their duty," she speaks carefully, "to care for the children till Mr. Hesse returns from Oregon. They say not good for white children to live with native woman alone."

A sorry kind of duty they've taken on themselves, I think. How stupid. Morning Bird's far better qualified to take care of them in this wilderness.

"But why are you here?"

"*Momook*," she says in Chinook, meaning work. I look at Thomas. He shrugs his shoulders.

"*Kloochman* is strong. Carry own pack, travel good in snow, no long

165

face. Just hungry all time. Me too," he says and laughs his tee-hee laugh. So we feed them some bacon and beans and when we're finished, the woman dons furs and boots and goes outside to clean the plates in the snow while we light our pipes. And it's while she's gone and we're smoking our pipes that Thomas tells us he's just come back from the Tait village at Yale, after visiting his sick father.

"He well again. Just like *lemule* . . . too stubborn to die." He laughs. "Yale gone bad. I leave quick. Miners drink plenty *tanglelegs*, get drunk, shoot guns, throw knives. Make much trouble. Two of my people, Tait, die in saloon the day I go, and a big *Oihe* go jail, then he die too."

There are not many Islanders here. We're all big men, and stand out wherever we go. "What did he look like?"

"No see."

"How did he die?"

He makes a slashing thrust across his chest. "He lived few moons with Tait *kloochman*. The woman catch his sickness. Is why men fight. *Oihe* set out for the Cariboo, but happy in Yale so stay long time. Big drunk."

"Do you know his name?"

"Hoo Hoo. Good name for a Chinaman."

"Ahuhu!" Moku says. "I'll be damned. Good riddance."

I take a deep breath. The man's been dead for a time, yet my hate for him has lived on. I should revel in the news of his death, but feel numb. It's good Ahuhu can no longer inflict pain on another human being, but the pleasure I thought I'd feel when he died, that escapes me. Instead, I feel as if I've lost something. This shames me, the sense of being incomplete without hate to feed upon. Thomas diverts my thoughts by passing me the pipe and says the Hawthorns sent Morning Bird away because of Nelson, Mr. Hawthorn's younger brother.

"He talk marriage. Want to live with Morning Bird till the father return from Oregon, so they take children, pay her small wage and tell her go, you leave. She say no to marry, but they take her in *chick chick* anyway, to 150 Mile and *whaah*! I find her there looking for you."

"Nelson wanted to marry Morning Bird? He's too young for her."

"What does that matter?" Moku says. "There's so few women around, and she's a damn fine looking woman, smart, capable too. She'd be an asset to that family."

"The boy's green as grass, naïve as they come. Morning Bird has seen lifetimes of hardship. What do they have in common?"

"Survival," Moku says abruptly, and it's true, so I say no more. The woman comes back in, so we revert to our pipes. It's the only time we smoke, when Thomas comes. And when he goes, it somehow comes about the woman stays to cook and clean for us, so we three can dig. It's accepted, as if discussed and agreed to, although it wasn't. She declines to occupy any of our rope beds, and sleeps on the floor on a bedroll till Zeke makes her one, with a blanket hung from the ceiling for privacy. She works hard, complains little and is no trouble, except having a woman's presence around reminds me of Rose. Zeke treats her with respect and Moku makes her laugh, but she and I remain awkward with each other.

The thaw churns the earth into oozing mud and with every step we sink calf deep in muck but we've waited long enough and are anxious to get started on the hunt for gold.

Moku and I try panning, with Zeke's help, and find that this is the easy part.

"Jes shovel dirt and gravel in the pan, set it low in the water and swirl it around in circles so's any large stones git thrown out. Break up the dirt with yore fingers, an' tip the muddy water and sand mix outta the pan. What's left in the bottom is black sand an' gold. You git a magnet to attract the black sand; what's left is gold. Thas all there is to it." But there is more. He heats his pan over the fire to dry the concentrates and sets the pan I've been using aside.

"Hold this," he says, and goes into the shack, returning with a sheet of brown paper off the oat box we bought at 150 Mile. He unfolds it and spreads the dried concentrates on the paper. Gold doesn't respond to magnetism but the black sand takes on life and creeps up the magnet. He dumps the sand aside, repeats the process again and again, then gently whuffs the last dust grains away with a soft puff of his big lips. And what's left is gold, fine dust, on the paper.

"I'll be damned," Moku grins. Zeke uses the back of his knife blade to scrape it into a small pile.

"We need somethin' fer storing it," he says, and I fetch a small jar from the shack and he creases the paper and gently tips the dust into the jar.

"How much do you reckon? A couple of ounces?"

"A tetch more. Good fo' a first time. This ain't the only way to git gold, though." And here he takes out the cans of lye and quicksilver he bought at 150 Mile, and a chamois cloth and some lime we brought for an outhouse not yet built. We dug a pit in the bush instead and throw lime on it when the shit freezes in heaped piles until we have to dig a new one. Zeke takes my pan of water and concentrates, and adds some lye and lime. He works this through the sand, then dunks the pan in water to wash the mix away. He pours a little quicksilver into the pan, rolling the pan around till the quicksilver forms a little ball and picks up all the gold dust. He lays the chamois cloth on some sand, makes a dent in the centre and puts the quicksilver into the hollow. He dumps the pan, fills it with water, and squeezes the quicksilver out of the chamois, holding it below the water so it won't splatter.

"We burn away the quicksilver that's left an' we git our gold. But we need a hotter fire for that." So we leave it for now. "Ah seen old timers use a potato for this," he says. "You half it, scoop out one side for the amalgam, press and wrap the halves together again firm like, and bake. You squeeze the potato to drain the mercury. But the chamois works better." I'm impressed, but the process takes longer than I imagined. Now I know we did the right thing damming the creek and building the flumes and sluice box to bring the water where we want to dig. Thanks to Zeke. It'll be ten times faster than panning, for sure.

Feeling responsible that Diego's brother José now has to work their claim on his own, we decide to offer him access to our water, on condition he help do the work of raising our dam and attaching his own box and flumes, under our supervision. But he's not around to take us up on our offer. We don't know if he's left for good, or if he'll be back. Meantime we've begun to shovel dirt and gravel into the box on top of the open wooden trough. It gets washed down the length of the sluice by the flume's stream of water. Beneath the box is a sloping surface Zeke covered in blanket, the "apron." Fine gold and sand wash through the holes in the box and get caught by the ridges and blanket on the apron. Mud and rock chunks wash out the lower end, leaving any gold behind. It's not difficult, but this too is hard work.

"Don't shovel too much at a time," Zeke warns, "or you'll cover the riffles and we won't ketch all the gold." So we settle on half shovel loads. It's raining so hard, the hems of our clothes feel like razors, chafing our skin with every move. But we shovel and shovel, drenched and miserable, till Zeke checks the apron, and throws his big arms in the air and hollers "We done it! We got gold!"

We plod laughing through the muck to reach him, mud sucking on our boots, and he drops tiny shiny nuggets into our hands.

"How much, do you reckon?"

"Forty, fifty dollars, maybe." Zeke says. "But there's the dust there too, worth somethin' when we separate it." And we can't stop smiling, for this is just one day's work. Suddenly we don't care about the rain or cold or the long winter we've been through. The dream's come alive.

Morning Bird celebrates with us, concocting a fish soup from dried salmon, adding beans and some green shoots she's dug up, as well as dried herbs from her own store. She cooks bannock the Indian way, with a thick batter made using bacon fat, winding it around a clean stick and cooking it over the fire. It's delicious. Gold must give you an appetite, for we eat like starved men.

Next day we work all day and find nothing. And the next day, and the next. There's talk of gold being found on bare rock in the Cariboo, but it's sure not where we're at. We work to the point of collapse for days on end but still nothing. Then Amundsen comes by and tells us that's normal, that he's taking out a hundred dollars some days, but some days nothing. So we keep digging.

Spring's come in like a slow-moving stream and the weather's warming. Life is sprouting around us. Morning Bird disappears from time to time, returning with green shoots she roots up to add to our meals. When we complain of sore muscles, she makes us tea from red willow bark, and our aches and pains disappear. And when we get colds, she rubs our chests with goose grease, and we get well quickly.

I don't dream so often of Rose, but one night she comes unbidden and I shout out when the old nightmare returns. Morning Bird pulls her blanket screen aside and slips into my bed and places her fingers on my lips. My mind's misty with memories and I've been celibate so long, it's easy to pretend she's Rose, that this is a dream conjured by my body's need. The woman says nothing, but wraps herself around me, skin warm as fire-baked stone, and I seize her like a man thirsting in the desert. I crush her till the breath goes out of her but she clings and moves with me and I lose myself. And when I see her lying spent upon my chest, so much longing for Rose wells up in me still, I'm hit with regret and a sense of coming injury to Morning Bird that I can't prevent. When I wake, she's squatting by the fire cooking porridge with a stick. Moku and Zeke say nothing, but must have heard our night's activity. Zeke's already outside and Moku's fixing our tapers, snipping the tallow wicks. I feel awkward around the woman, but she's busy with chores and doesn't look my way. Silence reels itself out and

I feel a tension round my chest that refuses to go away, for surely I must say something, but I don't.

We spend the day shovelling and luck's with us. Zeke hollers as three small nuggets show up on the apron.

"There's more than a hundred dollars here," he whoops.

"Not quite the fortune some are making." Moku frowns.

"Maybe we won't make a ton o' money," Zeke says. "But we kin make enough for this aw to be worthwhile."

He's right. Many creeks are mined out already. We can't afford to partner in those big joint ventures using expensive equipment to dig deep shafts, but we'll take what we can from the creek with the work of our backs as long as we can find some nuggets, or till we get tired of digging. So we dig, and shovel, and hunt for the glint of gold in the apron, and some days we find something, other days there's nothing. But before April's out, we reckon we have a thousand dollars in nuggets and dust. That's more than three hundred apiece. By the end of May, we've stashed away nearly three thousand, give or take.

In June Zeke shoots and skins a deer that wandered from the bush into our campsite. We butcher the animal for food and Morning Bird scrapes the hide, rubs it with the deer's brains, dries and tans the hide, then cuts and sews pouches for our gold dust. They're perfect containers. Better than the glass jars. What we don't eat of the deer, she dries and smokes for later.

She never returns to my bed, though we eye each other, exchanging silent messages neither of us can read. I sometimes wonder if I dreamed the encounter that night. I find I'm at a loss for words in her presence — acting like a fool youngster instead of a man over forty. I'm glad she's with us, though. She's not hard on the eyes either, slim and pretty as she is. Nor does she prattle the way some women do. I care for the woman, but I have plans and she doesn't fit into them.

With the dry weather, we've built our fire outside and sit there in the evenings discussing the day's work. Moku's in the shack, wrapping his knee after tripping over a boulder at the dam. Zeke's mending flumes so I find myself alone with the woman.

"Tell me about your wife," she says, speaking softly, the way Indian women can do. No sharp curiosity in her, just a quiet "Tell me."

"Her name was Rose," I say and take a deep breath. It's hard to talk about, it's been so long, but I tell her of the bear attack, and how Rose died. Morning Bird's dark eyes pool with tears. "Sorry," she whispers and lays a hand on mine. Then she rises and walks away, and it strikes me for the first time that her loss must be even greater than mine: a child dead as well as a spouse. I feel humbled by her fortitude and touched that she cries for me. We don't speak of it again, and except for that one night, she has not been in my bed.

The awkwardness between us lessens though, and the four of us go about our daily chores in rising spirits. The land is warming. The thin sunshine feels good on my Kanaka skin, triggering a longing for Oahu and for the warmth and aloha of the Islands. Meantime we keep digging and shovelling. Not every evening, but every second day or so, I help Moku and Zeke with their reading and writing. We've run out of the white paper I packed with me. Thomas is fetching a new supply next visit, but meantime we're using the brown wrap off our food packages. Morning Bird keeps house, digs for roots, cleans and cooks and sews and mends, all with a quick smile. At day's end, she helps Zeke separate gold from the concentrates. She's a quick learner and does whatever's needed without complaint.

I watch her ripening under freedom, like a piece of fruit on a tree, warming from the inside, expanding under her skin. She grows easy with us, and one night scolds us for not wiping the mud from our boots when we enter the cabin. Zeke mutters "Where did the slave woman go?" and we all laugh, including Morning Bird. Her laughter is clear, like the sound of bells at the old mission, her voice a light thing. Her indigenous calm defuses all our vexing complaints. I like having her around. Zeke and Moku have figured that out, for they go walking from time to time in the evenings when I'm not teaching them to read, leaving me alone with her. We only talk, but I look forward to the private times we have together.

Our diggings are paying off. By July, by our own reckoning, we've made nearly ten thousand dollars. It'll need to be assayed of course, but that's more than three thousand apiece.

"What will you do with all your gold?" Morning Bird asks Zeke.

"Set up shop somewhere an' be the boss man. Mendin' shoes or maybe smithin'."

"I'll buy land near the Fort," Moku says. "I like growing things, so I'll farm. And buy myself a Thumbbuster."

"And you, Kimo?"

I don't know what to say. I want land, but still don't know where. I'm growing fond of this woman, but she shouldn't hold any false hopes about a future with me. I don't want to hurt her though, for she's been hurt enough already. But I'm not ready for a commitment. Maybe she might be, though. So I play it safe.

"I'm buying land too. Most likely in Oahu. I'm hankering to go back and I'd have enough money to take Kami with me now." This is no lie, for though I've thought of homesteading around Langley, the notion of a new beginning back in the Islands still appeals to me. There at least I'd never be "Cariboo cold" again. Moku's one eyebrow lifts quizzically into a question mark. I feel like he's looking through me.

We all agree on one thing. We'll work through summer and leave before winter sets in. And though it's hard to know when enough's enough, we'll have dug all the gold we need . . . not as much as some, but enough because Moku misses Khatie and Keiki, and I miss Kami. And we're ready to go home. Zeke doesn't have a home, but he's had enough; he's itching to move on. The diggings are drying up around us.

It's what we figured; only the big machines will find deep gold now. But even if it was lying on the rocks just begging to be lifted, we'd still be leaving. There's not enough gold in the world to make us spend another winter in the Cariboo. Though there are men here — like Amundsen, strong-willed and adaptable — who thrive, and we wish them well.

When Thomas calls on his next trip, I give him a note to mail at whichever town he's next in, addressed to MacKay at Langley, asking him to let Kami know I'm coming home soon, and enclosing a note for him to read to Khatie from Moku, who boldly prints his own signature this time. Zeke says he needs write nobody. Thomas has a message for Morning Bird. They talk at length before Morning Bird nods and walks away, leaving us all curious as hell.

I haven't dreamt of Rose in months, but she comes, walking in and out of my mind as if it were our cabin in Langley. I tell her I'm going home. "Where's home?" she says, and disappears. I still don't know the answer.

The days are long now and the land is really heating up, but digging doesn't get any easier because we work later at night. The sun rises and sets, bringing blue skies and bright sunlight, leaving each day as cluttered and busy as the last. The heat intensifies till all green things stoop and bend to the ground. It's hot as the tropics, and we sweat buckets, tire quickly, and fight blood-hungry mosquitoes and flies that swarm over us like a flock of blackbirds. It can be beautiful though, this Cariboo, when the sun is roosting above the trees like a flaming orange, shining high, with no slow seeping away of light into dark.

All sorts of birds fill the sky: gulls, ducks, geese, swallows, ospreys, bald eagles, blue herons, woodpeckers. One day we stop digging to watch a flock of white swans fly overhead, the first I've ever seen. Zeke tells us they're trumpeters, and claims another odd white bird with a bag-like mouth is a type of pelican, as in his American south.

Morning Bird thinks, except for winter, this is a good place to live, with so much food at hand. Moose, deer, bears — both black and grizzly — make this place home, along with mountain goats, caribou, beavers and otters. We've even spotted a red fox.

Then one day Thomas arrives at our claim with two men in tow. One is a fine-looking gentleman, a banker named Theodore Hall. The other's a gaunt, weary-looking miner named John Wales. They've paid Thomas to take them to Barkerville. Folly, I think, for the trail is well travelled and they only have to follow their nose to find it. Drenched in sweat, Mr. Hall is wearing a fine suit and high-collared shirt, now grubby, that some Barkerville Chinaman will charge him a hefty fee to clean. He's a sturdy, serious little man, solidly built with a strong jaw and determined expression. Reminds me of our ship's captain on the boat from Hawaii, a man used to being in command.

Mr. Wales, it turns out, is an artist. Or was, before he took up mining. He's married to Mr. Hall's sister. Seems he came to mine but never found gold enough to cover his stake. His claim's not far from ours, along Beaver Creek, but he must've been hibernating when we passed, for we don't recognize him. Thomas found him for Mr. Hall, who has business in Barkerville, and he's taking his brother-in-law with him, under his wing so to speak, for the sake of his sister having food on her table and a husband returned alive, if not rich. I reckon Mr. Wales wasn't making a big living from his art or he'd never have tried mining in the first place. But I may be wrong. Gold draws every kind of man. He's tall, thin as a shovel, with fair hair and blue eyes and a sharp nose, and jaws that sink slightly into his face. He has a distant look, as if his mind's elsewhere. He's an odd soul, with a crooked half-smile, as if he's amused with something he sees that the rest of us don't. When they stop for coffee with us, Wales takes out a paper pad and starts to sketch Thomas.

"If he spent as much time digging as drawing, he might've found more gold," Mr. Hall mutters. Which may be true, but doesn't need saying in the man's hearing. I think Mr. Hall intends to return his brother-in-law to the ranks of dollars and employment. Mr. Wales plans to sketch all he can in Barkerville, while Hall's conducting business there.

"What'll you draw there, Mr. Wales?" I ask.

"The scenery, the people, the town itself."

"And can a man earn a living at this?" Moku asks bluntly.

"I expect to. Houses, restaurants, hotels, all need art work," he replies, though I doubt there's much call for art among miners. But then again, they're not all rough cut. Some are educated, refined gentlemen. Maybe there could be a market for his work.

"History's being made there," he says. "And you don't often get a chance to catch it when it's happening." His pale blue eyes are out of focus, as if he's checking something over my shoulder far off, out on the horizon somewhere. And it hits me, and my thoughts explode in pieces like the colours in a kaleidoscope, that he's looking ahead to a time when everyday living in the Cariboo will seem romantic, a golden time, a place of heroes and villains, as in epic tales of old. And I can feel my pulse leap.

"Why don't we go too, Moku?"

"What for?"

"To see it," I say. Because I'm feeling what Wales is feeling. And because I've been feeling empty, and I could use some distance from this shack, a gap in time and space to separate myself from the pitiless routine of digging twelve hours a day, and shore up in myself the reason I'm here. "We're this close. We should go. Wales is right. History's being made here, and we're living it." I'm grateful to the painter for opening my eyes.

"I can't trek. My knee's swollen like a melon," Moku reminds me. He stumbled over another boulder at the dam site. Twice he's done that now. Same knee.

"Ah'd like to go," Zeke says.

"Go then, the two of you. I'll stay. Morning Bird and I will mind the camp."

So just like that, it's settled. His knee will have time to heal while we're gone.

"Just stay away from the dam," I caution him. He doesn't need a third whack on that knee. He could use a few days' rest to let it heal, and Morning Bird will keep him company. I feel a pinch of something like envy.

At midday, Zeke and I head north with Thomas and his two clients. It's a clear fine day for trekking along Beaver Creek to the Quesnelle River. We head east to the Forks and Mr. Wales is taking in every detail of the landscape. He makes rough drawings on a pad as we pass the first big mine and sketches the giant Cornish wheel. Then his pencil brings to life the dirt piles, littered mine debris and the ugly maw of gouged-out earth.

"Why bother with that mess?" I ask.

"Because it's real," he says.

I thought pictures were meant to be pretty, bringing beauty to the world, depicting fine scenes or fine people. But to portray what's ugly because it's real? That makes me think; and what I think is, Mr. Wales has a gift to make men see the world through different eyes. I remember another picture, one at the Mission in Honolulu, of the bleeding Christ nailed to the cross. That wasn't pretty either. I've never thought much about art, but I understand now that it can have a voice.

chapter fifteen

THIS TRIP NORTHEAST IS a far cry from the winter trek I made earlier to the Forks, blanketed by snow and silence. Now the land is green, bird cries fill the air and there are flowers galore. Purple ones that Mr. Wales calls asters that look a lot like fleabane, and shiny buttercups glittering on the rocky slopes, cow parsnip growing shoulder-high along the ditches, and wild raspberries, the kind Morning Bird gathers and dries. There's goldenrod and lupines along the trail, and kinnikin-nick in its red berry stage. The grouse love it.

Mr. Wales fills pages of his sketch pad. We sleep in the open under the August moon, in our bedrolls. We don't need a fire but build it for comfort, as well as to keep the bears and wolves at bay. It doesn't stop the mosquitoes gorging on us though. They land in black clouds, bit-ing every piece of exposed skin till we're obliged to smear ourselves with a mix of tobacco juice and pennyroyal. This repels the mosquitoes, but the stink forces the gentlemen travellers to move to the far side of the fire.

Next day we set out again for the Forks, and when we arrive, we find an eating place next to the saloon at the entrance to town. There's a dog chained up outside. I recall the tied raccoon that was devoured when I was last there, so hope the dog will still be alive when we get back. As soon as we've eaten, we head out again. To reach Barkerville, we'll have to follow the trail along the Cariboo River to Keithley Creek. The banker's feet are giving him some pain so we stop to rest a spell. While Mr. Hall rests, Thomas directs us off the trail to some rock formations, like tall stone totems old as time, called hoodoos. The rock has eroded and weathered over time, leaving layers of different colours that I can't find a name for. Terracotta, the artist says. He's thrilled, and fills five pages. Myself, I feel like an intruder in some sacred place. And I'm relieved when we return to the trail through the tall pines drooping with fresh cones and filling the air with heavy scent.

We backtrack to pick up Mr. Hall, continue our trek along the Cariboo River and arrive at Keithley after dark. It was here Doc Keithley struck it rich, just months after Dunlevey found gold on Little Horsefly Creek, setting off the Cariboo rush. Now Keithley's nothing but a row of sad-looking thrown-together shacks, with a few miners milling about with glum faces. The creek's mined out, though it made a fortune for its namesake and other early prospectors. We camp above their hill, and leave early morning for Richfield, after the artist has sketched the long row of dilapidated shacks. It's taken us three days to get here. Longer than I figured, but Mr. Hall's really fighting his bleeding feet, the price for wearing fine expensive socks inside hard new boots. We have to stop often.

Mr. Wales wants to sketch all the creeks made famous in the Cariboo: Antler, Beggs Gulch, Canadian, China, Cunningham, Downy, Guyet, Lightning, Lowhee, Nugget Gulch, Quartz, Grouse, William's,

Wolfe and others. There's not a man in the Cariboo can't list them. And now we're close to Antler, named for the big antlers the first miners found on its bank, where gold lay on the ground for the picking. "We're not going," says Mr. Hall. "There's nothing to see. Antler's mined out. My contacts won't wait indefinitely and I'm already late." He has a tongue like a wasp. The man must've been raised on sour milk. It's his bleeding feet that are holding us all to this slow pace. But we walk on, and there'll be no sketches of Antler on Mr. Wales' pad. I don't know if he'll stay long enough to find all the places and faces he wants to sketch. The banker will surely have a say in that. You can always count on the crusty rind of truth being pointed out by a soul with no imagination.

The trail's busy with people coming and going: white men, Indians, even a few Chinamen. We scramble down the last hill of the gulch. Flumes criss-cross the hillside and Richfield pours open below us on the valley floor. When "Dutch Bill" Dietz and partners found gold, they named William's Creek after him. Then Ned Stout found gold at Richfield, and the town that sprang up was named because its rich gravel yielded more than one thousand dollars a foot.

Richfield's like every mining town, rows of shacks lining two sides of Main Street, about sixty or seventy of them. The place is buzzing. The saloons are packed. The stores are busy. There's a long lineup of miners outside the new gold commissioner's office. Talk is they're getting their own government buildings soon, and a jail and a courthouse and barracks for police. Richfield feels important, as if it's on the way to becoming something big.

We head for the saloon. The bartender tells us Judge Begbie lives here when he's in the Cariboo, in a one room cabin along the street. I can't imagine the aristocratic government official we met living in such a place, but it seems he does. We pay for our whiskeys, while Mr. Hall fumbles with his wallet.

"You Hawaiian?" the bartender asks. "One o' your kind was killed here two days ago in a shootout. Body's behind the constable's office waiting for identification. Maybe you'd know him? Don't see many of your kind up here," he says.

"It's your civic duty," Mr. Hall points out in his commanding banker's voice, "to see if you know him." Mr. Hall enjoys responsibility, wears it like a coat. He's right though, of course, so we trundle over to the find the constable. The constable's a tall, square-faced young man, thin as a reed, with long bow legs you notice the moment he stands up. I'm about to introduce myself when Mr. Hall takes over.

"Good day, constable. My name's Hall. I'm in the banking business, passing through with a Hawaiian friend, who might be able to identify the body you're holding. We felt it out civic duty to offer assistance." If Hall was the only banker I'd met, I'd have a low opinion of the profession, but I've met others in Langley a whole lot more polite.

The constable leads me behind his shack. A rough pine coffin box sits balanced across two old sawhorses. He opens the lid and pulls down the piece of white flour sacking covering the brown Kanaka face.

"He has no papers on him, nothing to say who he is, or where he's from."

The man's face is seamed and pock-marked, with ears sticking out like cauliflowers. His long black hair is speckled with grey. It's matted and parted at the crown and it's pulled behind his ears and lies over his shoulder in a long tail, tied with a dirty piece of string. There's no guessing at his age.

"I can't help," I say, when I find my voice. "I don't know him. Can I be alone with him for a moment?"

When the constable leaves, I chant a short funeral *melé* for this man, a fellow Islander, lost to his family, lost to his home. A man ought to have a name when he's buried. The dead McGregor had his name. So did Diego. It grieves me there's no knowing what this man's name is. In the old days in Hawaii, for a soul to rest, a man had to be buried where he was born. But a nameless Kanaka will lie here in this cold pine box in this cold land, and who can know if his soul will ever find its way home?

And so now I think of Ahuhu, that dark soul. The world's a safer place without him, but there was no joy for me in his death. It's hard to lay down a bundle you've nursed and kept warm for so long . . . but the bundle was hate, and today, I put that away from me. Ahuhu led a brutish life, always lusting after bad, at war with the world and everything in it. He made the rod for his own back. Heaven knows if a black soul like his will ever find peace. But now my ancestry calls me, and I chant a short funeral *melé* for Ahuhu's lost soul as well.

"Just call the man Kanaka," I tell the constable when I return. He writes it laboriously on a sheet of paper.

If only there was an English teacher here for Kanakas. They had one years ago at the fort on the Columbia River. Men might not die like this man did, without a name, without access to information about the law about rights and obligations. If they understood where they fit in society, the quarrels and shootings that put men into coffins early might not take place. This applies to all people, of course, not just Kanakas. I'm thinking of Diego the Spaniard now. Different people from different lands are creating a new kind of society here, with no common roots, but with a common destiny and since English is the language and law of the land, it seems to me understanding it is imperative. At least it's one path to bridge the gap between the old worlds and the new. And might help keep men out of early graves.

With a few bold strokes, Mr. Wales makes a rough sketch of the coffin atop its sawhorses. He means no disrespect but I'm uneasy, and relieved when Mr. Hall suggests we move along, as he wants to visit the bank.

Mr. Wales finds plenty of faces to scribble onto his pad while Mr.

Hall stops in at a shack with the name "Bank of British Columbia" in white paint above the door. We wait for him, but my mind stays on the dead Kanaka, with a name no one knows. I'm sorry for the man. I can't do anything for him, but seeing him has made me more determined than ever to teach Moku and Zeke as well as I can. They're making good progress and are pleased with their learning, and so far haven't grown peevish with me over it.

But here's Mr. Hall leaving the bank and we must move on, for it's just a short hop down the road to Barkerville, about ten minutes' easy walking. Farther down the creek lies Camerontown, another ten minutes' walk. All three towns, if you can call them that, sit on one mile of the creek, one running into the other, with Barkerville in the middle. All three are pulling out gold enough to make your head spin, one mine as much as three thousand dollars a day.

Barkerville, when we get there, is one great mud hole. A city of tents and wooden houses built on stilts in a saucer of land. They've logged the hillside for lumber for the town's mines, shops and houses, so it's bare, and flash floods have run down and churned the road into a bog. Miners are swarming about like flies on the plank sidewalks, and there's as much buzz in this town as in Richfield. Maybe more. Because here Billy Barker's made himself half a million.

It's hard to navigate through the piles of muck and flumes and sluices but we make for the boardwalk. Mr. Hall yelps when his boot slides on a wet log. He ends up arms oaring, sitting stunned in a pile of mud, eyes shut, his mouth like a paper cut. Thomas and I haul him up wriggling, mud dripping from his clothes. It's got into his boots, so he shakes one leg then the other, but it doesn't help his disposition much.

"My God! This is a hellhole!" he sputters. "Where's the damn hotel?" Thomas and Zeke help him climb up on the boardwalk. Thomas points halfway up the street to the Barkerville Hotel. We make for it, and deposit the banker. He'll need a bath and change of clothes before meeting with the town merchants, so we leave him at the door with Mr. Wales, who's smiling, but fighting it. Anywhere else, a clerk might object to gobs of mud dropping on his floor, but it's Barkerville and the desk man doesn't bat an eye.

"You want *muck muck*, eat here. Good food," Thomas says outside the Wake Up Jake restaurant. There's no shortage of boarding houses. There's also a barbershop run by a black man named Moses. Wellington Delaney Moses. Zeke stops to visit while Thomas and I head for the Kelly Saloon. Sure enough, the hurdies are lining the bar. Barkerville's bubbling like stew. You get the feeling something's fermenting here, like yeast in bread. The place pulsates with energy.

There's so much hope inside these men, it oozes from their pores — makes them big gamblers. Like everything in the Cariboo, it's extreme. In every saloon it's the same, men playing draw poker, seven-up and other games. Young men with pink cheeks, and old men with layered necks of folded skin. They'll stay up all night gambling, red-eyed, till they run out of money. Chinamen too, playing chuck-luck mostly, and smoking opium, which isn't good for them, but it's legal so there's no stopping it. There's not much else to do up here. I doubt many packed in books to read. Mr. Wales joins us, having left his brother-in-law in a tub of suds.

"There's so much to capture. I want to get as much down on paper as I can. Faces in particular." He flips his sketch book through drawings of Indians, of miners, of trees, of mountains. There's a sketch of Morning Bird brewing tea. He's caught her expression, and something flips in my stomach. He leaves the page open while he talks with Thomas, and I stare at the sketch. I care for this woman. But I don't want her complicating my plans, so I've kept my distance. It's better this way. If I cared less, it would be easier to walk away when I'm ready to go, but I don't want to hurt her. She's been hurt enough in her life. Wales returns for his pad, flips the page and there's a rough sketch of Thomas squatting by our campfire. I think it's a good likeness.

"What tribe are you, Thomas?" Wales asks.

"Tait, from the south."

He flips back some pages making notes. "And this?"

"Dakelhne, from here."

Wales flips several pages showing half a dozen other Indian faces he's drawn.

"And these?"

"What place you find them? Maybe Nlaka'pamux, Stl'atl'imx, Secwepemc, or Tsilhqot'in." While Thomas reviews the drawings, Wales scribbles notes for each face. I leave them, and head back along the sidewalk to find Zeke, and take in the town.

There are restaurants, boarding houses, hotels, saloons, brothels, a bakery and some shops run by Chinamen, with pigs and chickens running out back and a strong smell of opium in the air. Mr. Wales will find interesting faces among the shopkeepers here. A few doctors have hung up shingles. There'll be plenty of sick miners for them to tend, and bullets to dig out as well, I suppose. I never saw so many kinds of people in my life, speaking so many different tongues. There's rough men you'd want to avoid, and broken men down on their luck, run out of money and grub. There are educated gentlemen like Mr. Hall, and miners that struck gold, and men breaking their backs digging it for others for eight dollars a day — a high wage, if keeping fed up here didn't soak up half it. And there's merchants, making money off them all.

Zeke's still talking with Mr. Moses in the barbershop. When they see me through the window, Zeke waves me inside. Turns out Moses moved from San Francisco to Victoria in 1858, and came to the Cariboo recently to set up this barbershop and dry goods store. It's clean and orderly. The owner dresses as fine as any merchant I've set eyes on. He's soft-spoken, with intelligent eyes, a man who doesn't miss much. A bottle on a nearby shelf catches my eye. I take the top off, sniff it and peer at the label. *Hair Invigorator, to restore hair that has fallen off or become thin . . . relieve the Headache, and give the hair a dark and glossy colour.* I'll buy it for Moku, whose hair is still doing its rooster thing since he sneezed during Zeke's last haircut.

We take our leave and walk to Camerontown, about fifteen minutes farther down the creek. It's no town after all, just a row of houses John "Cariboo" Cameron built for the seventy-five men working shifts in his mine. We can't not visit this place though, since Cameron's the talk of the Cariboo, not just for his fortune, but for love of his wife Sophia, dead from typhoid, poor woman, not long after her baby died. After her funeral, Cameron buried her in a tin casket under his cabin. But he'd promised to take her home to Ontario, so when he did find gold later, he disinterred her coffin and, with his friend Robert Stevenson, strapped it to a sled, attached 50 pounds of gold dust to it, and travelled 600 miles on snowshoes and by horse and steamer, in -40 degree Fahrenheit weather, all the way south to Victoria, where he buried Sophia a second time, filling her coffin with alcohol to preserve the body. Finally in November, he disinterred the coffin and took Sophia home to Ontario, where she was buried for the third time.

"People don't believe she's in her coffin. They reckon he filled it with gold."

"I doubt it, Zeke. People fancy a conspiracy, but I don't believe it. Makes no sense to me." We walk the short length of Camerontown then trudge back to Barkerville.

We find Thomas and Mr. Wales still in the saloon, and take our leave. Wales is sketching the hurdies hovering beside a gambling foursome at one of the tables. We don't see Mr. Hall. He's either meeting with his merchants, or still scrubbing off the mud. I ask the bartender for two whiskeys. Zeke picks one up. I pick up the other, and we walk down the steps of the boardwalk to the street.

"Let's make a toast, Zeke. To Barkerville." We raise our glasses in the middle of Barkerville's muddy little street, and from out of no-where I think of Hopoo, my old teacher at the Christian Mission in Honolulu, intoning "I to the hills will lift mine eyes," and so I do . . . and I see not green, but brown hills, cross-hatched with flumes, piles of dirt and heaped-up mining debris. I see the brash row of wooden shack establishments lining this street, and I think of the stories that will be told of this place, of men like "Dutch" Bill, Doc Keithley, Billy Barker and the others, and of "Cariboo" Cameron and his Sophia, and of the Overlanders, and all those men who died for their dream. And I think about the people coming long after us, viewing this place from a different time, wondering about the glory days of the fabulous gold rush in this Cariboo, who will know nothing of its reality, or of the Kanaka Kimo and the Negraman Ezekiel, standing here now.

We finish our whiskeys and walk over to Wake Up Jake's for a meal before heading home.

"Ah won't ferget this place," Zeke says, "or the millions this creek is giving up. You hear the stories, but Ah can't git ma head round that kind o' money. Moses said there's three thousand claims staked along its banks but just forty are makin' fortunes. The Caledonian has pulled out $750,000. The Prairie Flower dug $100,000 in a day, Diller 102 pounds of gold in a day as well. Moses says big Bill Diller took out his weight in gold, 240 pounds of it, plus his dog's weight, 120 pounds, in jes a hundred feet of ground. Ma mind can't deal with numbers like that."

"If just forty are making it big, the rest are like us, Zeke, making a good few dollars a day, other days nothing. It's just the luck of the draw."

"Ah suppose. Luck's either with you, or it ain't."

"It's good we took over Guy's claim. If we'd come straight here, we'd have ended up digging for wages to pay our way home. And how long would that take us, with the price of food and lodging here?"

"We're better off where we are," Zeke says. Barkerville has settled our minds on that, and we head back in good spirits, feeling better than when we left. It's a fine trek back to our claim along the Cariboo River and the Quesnelle, and we don't hurry, for the Cariboo is a different, wild and beautiful place when it's not winter. Apart from the mosquitoes.

"Gittin' away done me a pile o'good," Zeke says.

"Me too." I'm rid of frustrations, and the threat of back-breaking last straws.

I hope Moku's knee has healed. With no digging and us gone, Morning Bird should feel rested too. I think about her now, how she's been an unforeseen surprise, how her presence has lifted the tedium of our long days, wrapping our dreary shack in her patient good nature. I'm looking forward to getting back.

When we reach Beaver Creek and our shack, we find Moku's knee is much improved and so is his disposition. He's whistling a happy jig, and he's finished mending some split flumes. He's rested up and in good shape. First thing he tells us though, is that Morning Bird has packed up and gone. I'm taken aback.

"Why? Where did she go?"

"Back to the Hesses. Nelson Hawthorn sent a message that the German had returned with his horses from Oregon and needs her to look after the children."

"I thought the Hawthorns were looking after the Hesse children?"

"They were. But they've done their duty, minding the children since the mother died, and they've had enough. Now he's on his own with them, and needs help so he can work his ranch. Said he'd take Morning Bird back. The children like her."

"So why did Nelson come instead of Hesse himself?"

"Maybe he didn't want to leave the children again. Nelson likely volunteered."

"Why didn't she wait till we came back?"

"What difference does it make?"

"She could've stayed to the end. Just a few more weeks."

"She'll see us at 150 Mile in September on our way back. We agreed to meet there on the first Saturday."

"Shouldn't we have paid her something?"

"I told her we'd figure it out and pay her some gold when we see her in September."

"You never know what that darn woman's doing, coming and going, turning up when you least expect it, and leaving the same way."

"Don't sound like the dog peed on the floor," Moku says. "Indians come and go when they please. You know that."

He's right. There's nothing to be said, nothing to be done. I'm rattled though.

We work through August, and reckon we've averaged around a hundred dollars a day on our claim, with the early months paying the most and recent efforts producing less and less. We're happy enough. We've made our stake and more. Much more. We'll have it assayed in town, but figure at $20 an ounce, we've made roughly $18,000, divided three ways gives us each about $6,000. We'll pay Morning Bird something, of course. It's not a huge fortune, but a mighty sum for an ex-slave and two former Hudson's Bay servants to share.

With Morning Bird gone, we take turns with the cabin chores.

"Ah'll cook," Zeke offers, but after Morning Bird's food, Zeke's tastes like boiled socks. We have to clean up after ourselves and do laundry again. It takes time away from the digging. Morning Bird used to help Zeke separate the gold from the concentrates at the end of the day. Now I have to do it. The cabin gathers clutter each day that passes, and we can't find things we're looking for. Vibrating with discontent, I complain to Moku.

"If she'd told us she was going, we could've organized things before she left."

"Like what?"

"You freed her, Kimo. She kin come an' go as she pleases," Zeke points out reasonably.

"I did, but not to run after a young whelp like Nelson Hawthorn."

"You told her you were going back to Oahu," Moku reminds me. "Why shouldn't she make a living for herself minding the Hesse children? She has a right to think of her future. Maybe Nelson will have something to say about that."

I'm peeved. Will he still want her for a wife, I wonder? But why should I care? I'm not ready for another woman. And yet I resent the thought of Morning Bird being with Nelson, or any other man for that matter. I miss her, and not just for her cooking and cleaning. It was a fine thing to watch her slave ways recede, and her self-assurance bloom, unfolding before us into something new and beautiful. And always, always there was that quick smile of hers.

The days feel long, as we count them down to month's end. We tell Amundsen we're giving up our claim, and sign it over to him so that he can register it for himself when we stop working it. He's happy, because our flumes are still in decent shape, and our cabin's bigger than his. He offers to pay for the claim, but we got it for nothing from Guy, who was planning to give it to the Swede anyway, so we decline his offer. Still, we accept payment for our cabin and flumes. Amundsen says he's joining a group of prospectors soon, so together they can afford the equipment to dig deep.

"Hide your gold for the trip south," he advises. "Get a poor-looking miner to carry it for you, or an Indian, to avoid being robbed, for there's so much thieving going on. The Barkerville miners all pack their gold with them to the mine each day then back to their shacks at night, for fear of it being stolen."

Our gold weighs about fifty-six pounds, so we split the weight between us. We'll hide Morning Bird's pouches in our clothing; the rest we stash deep in our packs.

The day we leave, dawn breaks imperceptibly, light seeping across the early-morning sky, blanketing the river. We pack as much on Fouter as the beast can carry. We finish loading our packs, strap around our waists the gold pouches Morning Bird made, and bequeath what's left to Amundsen. The trail back to 150 Mile looks like it's seen a war. Ravaged earth is gouged up in great heaps along with scattered rocks and gravel. Diverted streams have returned to their old beds, and dams are broken. Blasted holes, pits and dug-out caves litter the landscape, surrounded by broken flumes and bits of pipes, rockers and cradles. What can't be fixed has been left to rot. The makers of this mayhem are nowhere to be seen, the disappointed gone south and the determined off to join groups forming corporations to dig deeper mines. An era has fallen to bits around us.

We're among the lucky ones. We don't have to walk home. We're quitting the Cariboo with gold enough to pay our way. At 150 Mile, we'll take the coach south to Yale then board the steamer to Langley. It hurts that I'll have to leave the mule behind.

"We won't sell him to just any miner that comes along," I promise Zeke, who's as fond of old Fouter as I am. "We'll find somebody who'll treat him decent."

We pre-arranged a rendezvous with Thomas, and by the time he appears, I know what to do with the mule. I hand the Indian his reins.

"You keep him, Thomas, as thanks for your help. Treat him good, mind." The Indian's pleased. He should be. The mule cost me $100. Now, though, he's priceless. Thomas laughs and pats Fouter's rump.

"I take good care of *lemule*," he promises. I rub Fouter's coat, ruffle his bit ear and say my goodbyes. He gazes at me with his dark eyes, and I walk away from his blind trust. He's only a mule, I tell myself, only a mule, but my eyes are filling.

We're heading for the Barnard's Express ticket wicket, when Zeke says he's going to go all the way to Victoria.

"Ah liked the look o' thuh town. Gonna open me a barber shop like Wellington Moses done in Barkerville. There's plenty of ma people livin' there now." He means the thousand black Americans that Mr. Douglas invited to live as free men in Victoria.

But it comes to me, the provincial constable is hunting for a wanted man named Jeremiah Carter. If a man had a need to disappear, he'd have a better chance up here with constables few and far between than in a growing town like Victoria.

"Will you be safe down there, Zeke?"

"Ah should be." He looks me straight in the eye. "Ah'm gonna hang me a shingle and jes go about ma business."

He doesn't say, and I won't ask, if his real name's Ezekiel or if it's something else. I'll miss him. I believe he's a good man, a man of integrity. He'll find his fit some place, and I'm happy for him.

"So Moku, it'll just be you and me again."

"Not quite, *aikane*. There's the woman." And there she perches straight-backed on the split wooden bench by the Barnard's Express ticket office, dressed in her washed blue calico, head up, wide-eyed, her face looking like a box tied in a knot as if to say "Don't open." She's clasping her hands tight, her knuckles like small new potatoes. Beside her sits Nelson Hawthorn, turning his hat brim round and round nervously in his fingers till he catches sight of us and bolts to his feet.

"Hello, Nelson."

"Kimo. Moku. Good to see you." We shake hands.

"How are things going?" Moku takes the initiative.

"The farm's taking shape, though it's harder work than we figured." His skin is now a weathered brown, his fair hair turned blonder by the sun. His eyes are the same pale blue, but he's changed somehow

— stronger, in some indefinable way. It's the Cariboo. "I come up for supplies. Gave Morning Bird a ride."

No. There's more to this than giving Morning Bird a ride. I turn to her.

"Can we speak private like?" She rises to meet my gaze, expressionless still in her tight little bundle. She smells sweet, like trees after rain. Something comes up in my throat and my voice sounds stiff, stilted. "I hear you are looking after the Hesse children again."

"I did. But no more." She starts pressing out the wrinkles in her skirt with jerky movements of her small hands. I don't think she knows she's doing it.

"What do you mean, no more? Does Nelson still want to marry you?" I glance to the side. He's only a step away.

"Yes." She raises her chin ever so slightly, a hint of defiance? Pride? I don't know. Disappointment swamps me. Nelson Hawthorn's a decent man, but no match for a woman like Morning Bird. I want to tell her so. I want to tell her to wait, because I would make a better match. But wait for what? Till I make up my mind? I don't have the right. Or time, because she's here and she's leaving.

I've been in turmoil since she left us. I care for this woman, but marriage is a big step. I'd have to forget about returning to the Islands. But was that ever more than a dream? The yearning for Oahu I think will always be there, tucked away in the corner of my heart, where dreams end up after making way for reality. I'd have to stay. But Kami would gain a good mother, myself a good wife. We'd have money to buy land, to live a good life in this new society that's taking shape around us. Like Mr. Wales said, it's history being made, and we're part of it. Maybe I can teach English to the Kanakas around Langley. And to any others needing it to get by in this new world. There's surely a need for it. I think my old *kupuna* would be pleased.

Life necessitates many compromises. I was happy here with Rose. I could be happy again with Morning Bird. I know I don't love her as I did Rose, for youth calls for grand upheavings of passion and I'm beyond that at my age. Yet I love Morning Bird deeply in another way, no less real. It's different, but it's love all the same.

It's not easy to find the words I want to say. Her first language is Halq'emeylem, mine is Hawaiian, and we converse in Chinook and in English — a fine language for counting pennies and shillings, but not for what lies between a man and a woman. The question sticks in my throat.

"You've had a hard life, Morning Bird. Nelson's not the man for you."

"Because I'm Indian?"

"No."

"Because he's younger?"

"No. Because you need someone strong, someone who's been through the fire." I'm reaching now, plucking at possibilities like cherries off a tree. The words get trapped in my throat, but I push them out. "Someone like me."

I can't read her expression. Something jolts me, comes and goes in a flash. A flicker of dismay, or panic. I don't know. Maybe I'm too late.

"Mister Hesse, he hires new woman, Dakelhne, to help with the children when I leave," she says. Frustration grips me again and I feel a sense of dislocation, as if I've lost my bearings.

"When? When are you leaving?"

"Whenever you're ready," she says quietly, then sits herself back on the bench and looks up at me and smiles, a tiny thing, a leaf fluttering in the wind. I stand like a fool staring at her with a longing of so many kinds sluicing through me, I'm worried it'll all spew out.

"Are you saying yes?"

"I say yes." It's a whisper, but she's out of her tight bundle and smiling now, bubbling into a little chuff of laughter, cheeks rounding like small apples.

We don't embrace in public; it's not the Indian way. That'll come later though, in private. I feel like laughing out loud, but what I do is smile. I've missed this woman. I feel I'm on the edge of life, waiting for it to begin again knowing, as she must, that we've already begun to travel down a new road.

"You go Oihe?" she asks. I consider it for a split second only. Morning Bird has just found herself after years of slavery. She'd be lost in Hawaii. I don't want her to lose herself again. I shake my head.

"No. I'm staying. I need a partner, Morning Bird, and a mother for Kami."

"I make good wife," she states simply, then stands up. Beneath the wooden bench is her backpack bundle. Nelson reaches for it and hands it to me with a wry smile.

"Goodbye, Morning Bird. If I'm ever down in Langley, I'll look for you and Kimo." He shakes my hand. "Good luck," he says. "You win." And I think back to the gambler rolling dice in Hope, and yes, indeed I did. But it's something to hope for, and I do believe in this new world that's being built, that slavery will be a thing of the past, that no more Morning Birds will be used as pawns in a game of chance. That was a remnant of the past, the dregs of a waning way of life, best buried not to see the light of day again.

I feel good about what's ahead. Gold, I think, has forever altered life here, even if it eventually runs out, which it will. People from other lands, with new ideas and attitudes, are creating a different kind of society, where every kind of man can find a fit, and old walls of class and race are crumbling beneath the tide. Yes, there's much to feel good about.

We buy our tickets south and squeeze together into the Barnard's Express coach heading for Yale. I'm going home to Kami. Rose would be pleased I've kept my promise. I've said goodbye to her now. She understands. I'll buy land with my share of the gold, maybe in Derby, next to the fort. But still near Moku, who's whistling one of his tunes when he's not nodding off dreaming about his Thumbbuster.

Mile after mile we rumble south and I feel a sadness leaving that place, for the Cariboo has a terrifying beauty of its own. It has a wild majesty that holds great appeal for men who march to their own drum. And though I'm not staying, I appreciate the fabulous lunacy of those who do. Morning Bird, serene as a queen, gazes placidly out of the window while the coach's wheels eat up the miles. I've taken no great fortune from the Cariboo, no great Billy Barker strike, but have more than enough to build me a new life. With a new wife.

And that's good fortune enough for any man. And so I say goodbye to the Cariboo and the Cariboo gold. *Aloha*.

ABOUT THE AUTHOR

SUSAN DOBBIE WAS BORN in Edinburgh, Scotland, and educated at James Gillespie's High School for Girls. She immigrated to Canada in 1957 where she attended Simon Fraser University as a mature student, majoring in English literature. She has worked for many years as a docent at Langley Centennial Museum, during which she developed her interest in early Pacific Northwest life. Her first book of fiction, *When Eagles Call*, focused on the lives of Hawaiians hired by the Hudson's Bay Company in the mid-nineteenth century to work under contract at Fort Langley on the Fraser River. The sequel, *River of Gold*, is set during the tempestuous years of the Fraser and Cariboo gold rush eras, and once again centres on the Hawaiians and the native people. It is a time when men like James Douglas and Judge Begbie stepped forward to forge a country, when native life was almost unretrievably damaged, and when fortune seekers of every nationality mingled, lived, loved and died but ultimately shaped a new society — one that we have inherited. Now semi-retired, Susan Dobbie lives with her husband in Langley, British Columbia.

Marquis Book Printing Inc.

Québec, Canada

2009